RISE OF THE GEEKS FOLLOWING AN ALIEN INVASION!

JONATHAN HIPKISS

authorHOUSE®

AuthorHouse™ UK
1663 Liberty Drive
Bloomington, IN 47403 USA
www.authorhouse.co.uk
Phone: 0800.197.4150

Published by AuthorHouse   11/08/2016

ISBN: 978-1-5246-6404-6 (sc)
ISBN: 978-1-5246-6407-7 (e)

Print information available on the last page.

This book is printed on acid-free paper.

In loving memory of my dog Wicket,
The greatest and most loyal friend there ever was.
I miss you little brother.

"You're only given a little spark of
madness…you mustn't lose it."
- Robin Williams

"Through the years and miles between us,
It's been a long and lonely ride,
But if I got that call in the dead of the night,
I'd be right by your side."
- *Blood On Blood*

Written by Jon Bon Jovi,
Richie Sambora and Desmond Child
Taken from the album *New Jersey*

CONTENTS

PROLOUGE

THE LOST AGE OF INNOCENCE AND THE PURSUIT TO RECLAIM THE BEAUTY OF IT

Detroit, Michigan. 1957.

Lucy.

Just the thought of saying her name made his eight-year old, pre-pubescent mind go wild. He loved her, or at least he thought he loved her. That much was true. And she was the prettiest girl in school, a clear fact that was most definitely true.

Tommy Goodson would stare at her all day from his peripheral vision. Because he was left-handed, he had developed a little knack of twisting his body on his desk in order to give him in an even better view of his crush. When he put his mind to it, Tommy could get away with fifty minutes of staring per school day. *How did he achieve this?* His teacher had called him 'overtly-intellectual' and that was just by the age of five. So, theoretically, he could stare as much as he wanted at Lucy and still have the work done before his classmates.

Despite being a tender age, Tommy despised how fast he was growing up. Time was accelerating at a pace even he couldn't keep up with. Already he was aware of the goings on of President Eisenhower, he was acutely in tune with the events surrounding the Cold War and he took a mild interest in Sputnik. He absorbed all the information he was given, most importantly though, he retained it.

While he was a misguided soul when it came to social situations, the young Tommy Goodson was socially aware of the world around him. He understood what Martin Luther King Jr. was actively seeking in order to try and resist oppression, meanwhile his father wouldn't stop banging on about a company called Toyota that had just started selling its automobiles in the US and his mother would not stop yapping on about something called 'Graceland' in Memphis. She constantly began a dialogue about how it was the new mansion of Elvis Presley. While Tommy hero-worshipped the king of rock and roll, he didn't too much care for some house he lived in.

All the boys his age and older were obsessed with Elvis, and why wouldn't they be? It helped that Lucy loved him too but what didn't help was that Lucy's boyfriend looked like an identical twin to Mr. Presley.

Though little Tommy was a natural red head, that didn't stop him from trying to imitate the king's famous black mop of hair. One afternoon, a few months ago, Tommy found some black paint from the garage and poured it all over his hair, then erratically began to rub it in. The following morning was to be a lesson in sheer childhood embarrassment as his mother hadn't been able to wash it all out. At playtime the next day, he found himself being thrown in the dirt and mud by the older kids. It had been humiliating.

Still, he had Lucy.

It would be perfect, if only it wasn't for her boyfriend; Big Jimmy. Though Big Jimmy was the same age as Tommy, he was built like a teenager and was most definitely a bully. Little Tommy Goodson lived in fear of what Big Jimmy might do next.

The school bell rang. Tommy awoke from his daydreaming slumber and picked up his books to head to his next class. It wasn't to be; however, fore as he turned the corner, he was abruptly halted by the sight of Big Jimmy, Big Stevie and Eric. (Eric couldn't afford a 'big' before his name, as alas, his growth had been stunted at birth.)

"Where ya goin' little punk?!" Big Jimmy demanded.

"Class," came the meek reply.

"You're such a fuckin' little dork!'"

The fact that Big Jimmy had cussed was enough to draw pretty much the entire passing corridor of kids in to watch what was happening.

"I...just want to go to class."

"Don't' cha wanna play, punk?"

"No"

"C'mon, nerd! Bet ya got some nerdy shit in that bag, huh!"

Before Tommy could react, his famed bully snatched his rucksack and spilled the contents all over the floor. There, spew for all to see, was his homework assignments, the cotton wool his grandmother gave to him for protection and his beloved stash of comic books.

Now, comic books were one thing that Tommy loved more than anything in the world. He may have even loved them more than Lucy. Tommy read them all; Batman, Superman, The Flash, Archie, The Lone Ranger to name but a few. And they were now all exposed.

Big Jimmy simply laughed a belly laugh from deep within. "What a little chicken shit, geek"

Tommy's tormenter succeeded in kicking all of his comic books everywhere and then aggressively sent them flying over his head. Tommy had been saving his allowance for weeks to buy some of the new ones from the local store and now they were ripped and torn, forever lost to the trash can.

Feeling the bitter sting of humiliating tears come to his eyes, Tommy ran as fast as he could from the corridor and sprinted home.

Tommy burst through the door, quietly thinking that he was going crazy as he was adamant he could still hear the raucous laughter of the school children. He saw that his mother was outside in the garden talking to their neighbour, so he sprinted to the top of the stairs and aimed for his bedroom.

He stopped, fingers just on the door handle, and it was then he felt his heart rate had slowed and his breathing had returned to normal. He felt instantly calm again, knowing that he was about to enter his utopia.

He entered his bedroom and sighed happily. In one corner of the room lay stacks of comic books of all different genres. Tommy didn't care what they were, he just loved comics. On his window shelf were toy figurines of Davy Crochet and Mickey Mouse, the Disney toy a personal favourite from his most beloved cartoon, 1928's *Steamboat Willie*. Next to his toys were three model rocket ships of all different designs. Tommy loved to jump off his bed with the ship in hand and race around the house in a maelstrom of adventure.

Tommy's eyes then drifted towards his toy chest. He skipped over and unloaded its contents; hundreds and hundreds of toy soldiers. The ones Tommy owned were plastic because the Government, or someone like it, had recently decided that lead toys were not safe for children. Tommy had amassed a pretty impressive amount of soldiers, and it helped that sometimes they were on offer around Christmas time and the local store usually reduced them to two-hundred and four soldiers for one dollar and ninety-eight cents. *It had been a very good Christmas last year.*

These were his favourite games to play. In the comfort of his bedroom, Tommy was the master of his own universe. His soldiers could declare war or make peace or even go on special missions, such as a ride on a rocket ship. (Occasionally, a soldier would go on a date with his little sister's Barbie doll but Tommy didn't know too much about 'adult time' to know what the dolls were supposed to do after talking.)

Tommy loved making his soldiers become space men and would send them off on missions to far away planets to battle evil beings from another world. He often wondered what would happen if beings from a different planet would invade earth. After all, there were plenty of movies on the subject but his little brain thought about what would happen in real life. He knew that the US army would no doubt save the world but Tommy thought that it would take really smart people to think about how they were going to win. He knew that it would be the intelligent people, perhaps like himself, to find the resolution to earth's greatest problem.

And then he had it.

The perfect idea for what the story was going to be on his solitary afternoon. He quickly called his dog from downstairs that would act as the hairy, giant alien and set up his army of soldiers ready for the attack. He then took four figures and snapped off the weapons from each of them. These were going to be his 'clever people to really save the world.'

That was all he needed to be content; just him, his toys and his imagination. He didn't once think about the bullies at school or the homework he had to do or the fact that the girl he loved would probably never love him back. Tommy just sat there for hours in his bedroom and played with his toys. And so, it was there on that blissful afternoon, armed with toys galore, that little Tommy charted a rise of the geeks following an alien invasion. Little did he know, that one day, decades from now, his playtime fantasy would one day come true.

PART I:

MOCKED MISFITS

CHAPTER ONE

PRESENT DAY…ENGLAND…

6.30.am.

The alarm began its nasal like war cry.

Chilvers sighed. He'd been lying awake for almost half an hour whilst silently praying that 6.30 am would never come. Chilvers, like most of the sane community, loathed Tuesdays with a quiet passion. The weekend just gone was now a distant memory, while the prospect of the next weekend seemed like nothing more than a hopeful dream. Chilvers knew that if he didn't haul himself out of bed in the next few minutes, he never would at all today.

At fourteen years old, Chilvers stood at an impressive six-foot-one. His height, however, was already begging to take its toll. He astonishingly towered above the tallest girl at school and his feet and calves hung over the end of his bed. He didn't mind in the summer but the winter months were an ever growing pain with the possibility of frost bite an ever growing reality.

Minutes passed and Chilvers was still desperately willing his body to get out of his BO ridden pit. It was in these quiet moments in a morning that Chilvers would contemplate and collect his thoughts for the day.

His first thought was always a simple one: he desperately needed to change his Spider-Man bed sheets. The reason was obvious…the smell. No matter how many times Chilvers washed or used deodorant, he could not shake the smell of being a teenage boy and it was getting worse.

The second reason to change his sheets was a little more complicated…the prospect of bringing a girl into his bedroom and seeing his bed sheets absolutely mortified him. No matter how many times he thought that a member of the opposite sex would see his childhood sheets, he always consoled himself with the notion that a girl would probably never see the inside of his bedroom. Period. In fact, the only woman to see and handle the delicacy of his DNA ridden bed sheets was his mother and that just made him feel even more lonely and unwanted. Not to mention a little bitter in the mouth.

Chilvers noted of late that he had found himself in more down beat moods than usual. He didn't think he was depressed but considered the fact that he was becoming increasingly bored and frustrated by the monotony of life. All these unwanted, bleak feelings and he was only fourteen! The future of his emotional state did not look optimistic. His love of comic books, movies and toys brought him vast pleasure and joy…yet he knew…he needed…more.

This brought him to his next trail of thought; a semi-naked Harrison Ford.

Chilvers, like his best friends, spent a lot of time thinking about the Hollywood actor and demi-God that went by the name of Harrison Ford. He was after all, his hero, and Chilvers had devoted a lot of time and a lot of life into hero-worshipping the man. He followed his off-screen life closely and attentively with almost disturbing scrutiny. He followed his on screen career with such intensity, that Chilvers and his pals knew what movie Ford would sign onto next before Ford himself did.

When Ford had been in a plane crash in 2015, Chilvers had broken down weeping in his bedroom. Much to the concern of his father, Chilvers then took to lighting candles at his local church until official word reached the world that Harrison Ford would be okay.

Chilvers also had another reason to think of Harrison Ford every morning when he woke up…he had a half-naked poster of Ford taped to his bedroom ceiling.

It was a picture of Ford in full action-hero mode with a hint of a beard and ripped torso on full view. The poster had raised a few eyebrows when it first went up a few years ago. Chilvers' mother had told her son that she 'loved him no matter what'; meanwhile his father had led a family campaign for his son to come out of the closet 'as soon as possible.' It never helped that his older brother, Andy, who was as far removed from a geek as physically possible, was constantly parading girl after girl at the dinner table, each more prettier than the last.

Chilvers, who considered himself to be very much a heterosexual, had put the semi-nude poster on his ceiling for another reason and that was to simply give him inspiration. Inspiration to be a better person than he already was but more importantly for a teenage boy; inspiration to gain a better body.

A few minutes later and it was time for his daily morning workout. He rolled out of bed with a thud whilst maintaining his eyes in a semi-asleep daze. He lay there, motionless for a few minutes, and then braced his body ready for the excruciating torture of his workout. He strained his body to perform a sit-up, and then exhausted by this, collapsed back on the floor. Happy with the work accomplished, Chilvers picked himself up to get ready for school.

Andy usually took an unsettling amount of time in the bathroom, and so Chilvers very often had to beg his older sibling for a quick five minutes use of the shower. Like most teenage boys, he used this time wisely.

First order of business was to inspect his precious manhood. He had a quick glance down to see if it had grown in size but he was always left heart achingly disappointed. This was followed by a quick brush of the teeth and then the mammoth quest of trying to make some semblance of his aggressively shaggy hair.

With his teenage hygiene accomplished for the morning, Chilvers' inhaled and braced himself for another day of mediocrity.

The first onslaught of the day began with navigating the smokers outside the school gates. Chilvers had always wondered how kids his age could afford to light up as many of his peers who smoked came from working class households, much like himself. His answer to this long pondered question finally came to fruition in the form of science teacher Mr. Bellerby. Chilvers noted him handing out packets of cigarettes to the older kids in exchange for cash, all the while Mr. Bellerby kept note of anyone who was watching this sly interaction.

The next sight that met Chilvers' eyes every morning was the vision of the caretaker's shed. He had to pass it without fail as his locker was located the other side of campus. What took place behind the shed was a hive of pure teenage rebellious activity.

The testosterone fuelled teenage boys would persuade their partners to give them a quick fumble before class started. Chilvers loathed it. Not only did every class already bare a stench of unwashed arm pits but there was also a distinct aroma of sex in the air or failing that, there were simply some very questionable smells.

This particular morning Chilvers had arrived at his locker relatively unscathed but his fear of what might happen next was relatively incalculable. His locker was situated next to a student who went by the name of Wrecker Wayne. Most of the school presumed it was because he was always totally obliterated at any party that took place but Chilvers' mom had known Wayne's mother for years and Chilvers knew that the term "Wrecker" actually implied itself to a more personal, tender matter. Wayne knew that Chilvers was aware of his now delicate manhood and he seethed at the thought every day. Wayne's face was that of utter disgust whenever he laid eyes upon Chilvers, now known as the 'king of the geeks.'

"S'up, nerd," came the painfully obvious greeting. It was the same one every morning.

Chilvers didn't have it in him to argue or think of a witty comeback. He simply stated the obvious, "Morning."

"What comic books you been jerking off over this morning?"

"None."

"Or you been getting excited over pictures of your mum again?" Wayne was beside himself with hoards of laughter.

"No, actually. Those pictures of your sister are proving to be most advantageous." Chilvers allowed a sly, half-smile to form from his lips. He'd done it; he'd given an actual comeback. And a witty one at that.

Wayne's expression, however, was completely grief stricken. "Bro...that's sick...my sister's like...nine... and...disabled."

Oh shit, were the only words that came to his blank mind. "I...ermmm...didn't mean..."

The next words that left Wayne's mouth were enough to make Chilvers want to crawl into a tiny hole and dig his way to hell for eternity. "I will make sure everyone knows about this. Everyone!"

Chilvers simply thought what he felt. *Oh shit.* The day had barely begun and it was not looking like it was going to go his way. Only the arrival of a familiar and friendly voice was enough to shift him from his depressive daze.

Chilvers noted that Matt looked tired. His usual spring-like bounce was nowhere to be found this morning. His hair was more wiry than usual and his skin looked like it had been devoid of any kind of moisture for years. Matt was the epitome of a stereotypical bookworm if ever there was one. That had its advantages, of course, as he always carried an air of intelligence and forward thinking, alas, much like Chilvers, however, his social skills and funk with the ladies was pretty much non-existent.

"What happened to you last night?" Chilvers probed.

"I had a date."

Suspense hung in the air. Chilvers was simply stunned. "Wait…what? A date? How did it go? Who with?"

"Don't get too excited. I tried that internet dating thing. I put in all my personal details. I covered all my tastes from books, to films, TV and collecting memorabilia. In the personal quotes bit I put down that my aim in life was to become a 'Harrison Ford-type action hero'…or at least that's what I thought I put. Turned out it said that I wanted to date a 'Harrison Ford-type' companion."

"Oh, so what happened?"

"I went on a dinner date with an eighty-two year old gay man who looked more like my Aunty Shelia than he did Harrison Ford."

"Well, that sucks. So, you didn't get to touch a girl?"

"Nope, instead he made an offer …but I think his catheter may have gotten in the way. Not that I was thinking about touching, for the record. The whole thing was kind of creepy."

"Yikes, that's …some experience." Chilvers felt the need to comfort his friend. He searched for the right words. "One day, my friend, you will be with a woman, as will I. I promise." Was it a lie? Possibly. Chilvers didn't hold out any hope of ever sharing his life with a female companion. Or any companion for that matter.

One person who did hold out hope, however, was the third member of their dysfunctional clan.

Tom strolled briskly up to his friends with a demeanour of determination and self-serving arrogance. He was a small specimen, with a slight hunchback and wild, gangly arms. His eyes always seemed to be chasing his next thought whilst his mouth was still catching up from a few moments before. "Good morning, gentlemen," came his grand opening.

"Hey, buddy," the other boys replied in unison.

"I have news. Good news. I've been working on a project for a while and I think it's finally going to happen."

Matt rolled his eyes. He'd heard this before. Tom was always looking for his next adventure and was always up to some scheme or another to make it happen. His plans often fell by the wayside until one time, a few years ago; Tom had garnered the attention of the national press.

He was determined to meet his hero Harrison Ford and the only way he saw fit to do this was to declare it his last wish. *His dying wish nonetheless.* So, Tom proudly contacted a local charity to declare that he was dying and asked them whether they would be interested in sending him on a plane to finally come face-to-face with Ford. They happily obliged and it seemed to be working for a few weeks until finally the game was up and they then realised that he was an absolute picture of health.

Tom then resorted to his plan B; that he was suffering from some mental disorder that made him lie. It was

Chilvers who came up with the idea to tell the media that he was suffering from Munchausen-by-proxy. The press had gallantly eased off his case but doctors hadn't. Chilvers always reminded him that doctors doing tests for a while was a small price to pay to keep from being shamed by the country.

"So, what's this news?" Matt asked, quietly not wanting to know the answer.

"I'm going to sleep with a prostitute."

"Why?" Chilvers boomed, not hiding his horror and confusion.

"I'm going to lose my virginity."

"How are you going to do this?"

"I don't know."

"How are you paying for this?"

"I don't know."

"When are you going to tell your mother?"

"Already have."

Chilvers banged his head against his locker. "Sweet Jesus. What have we come to?"

"I would have loved to have been there for that conversation," Matt sputtered out, half laughing; half wishing that he had thought of the idea last night.

There they stood, an odd trio of misfits simply trying to find a place in the world. To outsiders, they all looked like they should be targeted as potential sex offenders but they were simply an individualistic bunch that were at the moment missing the fourth member of their group.

"Anyone seen Mark?" Chilvers wondered.

"Not since school finished last night," Matt replied. "Perhaps he's in the canteen."

Chilvers picked up his bag. "We better go find him. You know he doesn't do well by himself in social spaces."

*

Perth, Australia.

He'd always loved the ocean. Ever since he was a small child there was nothing else he loved more than hitting the beach and being in the cool, soothing water. These days, however, he came to the beach with different motives.

Gone were the years of care free play with his friends or long summer days spent with his father wondering about the future. Adulthood had tapped him on the shoulder a few years ago and he had been forced to unwillingly accept its invitation.

The sky had cast its blanket of darkness over the land and the water looked as inviting as ever. He sat himself down and gazed over the infinite sea. Up above, a vast array of stars seemed to be winking, as if just for him. At the age of twenty-five, Shaun found himself accustomed to these quiet moments of solitude. He longed to wade out into the water, and perhaps let the water drown his worries but tonight he sat alone and gazed up at the sky and wondered about the world in which he found himself in.

Was there a grand designer? Someone or something who had been the architect to this thing they called life?

If there was, then they must have been a very intelligent yet conflicted individual indeed. Perhaps the universe had a plan for him? If it did, Shaun didn't know what it was.

His gaze was eventually drawn to a school of fish. *Why had humans evolved into the dominant species?* Sometimes the actions of humans dumfounded him. War, betrayal, murder, the list was endless. Perhaps the universe was the complete opposite of what religion stood for. Perhaps there was no meaning, perhaps it was really just a bunch of random atoms swirling and colliding until a seismic event occurred.

Shaun suddenly felt aware of his mortality. He didn't like it. He hated to think that one day he would no longer be able to experience this moving sphere that people called earth.

He shuddered.

Suddenly, he felt his soul weighed down from where his trail of thought had led him. Shaun was very aware of what happened in a midlife crisis, his own father had suffered one with drastic consequences.

Perhaps he was suffering an existential crisis? Perhaps he was caught in a so called vacuum of nothingness and boredom. *Probably,* he thought. *And I need to forget about this.* Shaun checked his watch and concluded that if he left now, then he could arrive fashionably late to the party. *Alcohol is always a good remedy.*

Shaun picked up his bag and jacket and headed off back across the beach. He shook his head of such thoughts of cloudiness but as he did, he missed something in the sky behind him. He never saw the flash of light from up above and he was completely unaware of the rondure wonderment that shot across the darkened horizon with awe striking speed.

*

Chilvers, Tom and Matt sat down with their supposedly 'low fat' breakfast. The dinner ladies made questionable food and their hygiene was like something out of a horror film but then everyone knew what their wages were and no one could dare blame them for doing a subpar job.

The canteen was another minefield to navigate for the geeks as it was deemed another social hangout where the boys didn't belong. Like antelope at a watering hole, it was always going to end in disaster. The boys kept their heads down whilst a world of teenage angst unfolded around them.

Sat opposite them were a young couple in love, Hector and Shirley. Chilvers noted that their argument was becoming more heated and desperately avoided eye contact. Shirley was screeching at her boyfriend, seemingly breaking the decimal barrier in the process. "Get away from me, Hector!"

Hector seemed unfazed. He was clutching a beer in one hand, hidden in a small black bag, whilst his other hand was caressing his girlfriend's tragically home dyed hair. "But, Shirley, please, you is my bitch!"

The geeks all winced. They didn't know anything about women but they understood that calling your partner a 'bitch' was pretty much out of the question.

"You cheated on me, Hector, and I don't think I can forgive you," came her counter argument. "I love you, boy, but you is gonna have to realise that you is never gonna do better than me. Our love is written in the stars, so you best start treating me with respect, yeah?"

Hector didn't seem fazed by this; on the contrary, he looked like he was thriving off it. He rose from his seat and slammed his tray on the table. "Yeah, well I got something to tell you!"

"Oh, yeah, what is that?"

"I is cheating on you with your sister, yeah!"

Silence.

Shirley's face looked like she had just seen a recently deceased relative come back amongst the living.

The geeks buried their heads deeper into themselves. Watching personal drama unfold before them so early in the morning was not their idea of a good time. Thankfully, it evaporated fairly quickly as Hector stormed off in blind rage while Shirley darted after him.

Chilvers gave a pained expression. "Well, that was... interesting."

"After watching scenes like that, it makes me glad I don't have a girlfriend," Matt offered, knowing he was echoing the thoughts of everyone present.

Chilvers nodded. "Still no sign of Mark?"

"He hasn't text."

Tom waved his hand dramatically, like a veteran stage thespian witnessing a shambolic butchering of classic work. "Enough of this chit-chat! I have something far more interesting to discuss." Tom reached for his bag but abruptly pulled back when he saw a figure emerge from his peripheral vision. "Oh God."

"Look who it is! It's the fuckin' rejects!" The voice belonged to one of the older pupils in school and a known hard case or as Chilvers liked to call him, a bully. "What nerdy shit you girls talking about today?"

The bully was raising his voice loud enough just to draw attention from the rest of the canteen. This was beginning to happen all too often. The boys kept their heads down in hope the incident would pass over.

"We're just having breakfast. That's all we're doing," Matt meekly offered.

"Surprised you dicks ain't talking about that film bloke you love so much. Henry Fool or whatever his fuckin' name is."

"Harrison Ford," Tom shot back.

"What?"

"Harrison Ford," Tom raged again, this time a little louder. "His name is HARRISON FORD."

"Oh, so fuckin' what?"

Tom stood his ground. "He happens to be the highest grossing actor of all time and you may have heard of some of his films…*Star Wars…Indiana Jones…Blade Runner… Working Girl…?*"

14

Their towering bully looked a little taken aback by this little surge of courage from Tom.

Chilvers and Matt on the other hand, were simply terrified.

"Tom, sit down, you're making a scene," Matt cautiously warned.

Tom buckled up straight, as if hit by a jolt of energy. "Yeah, I am going to make a scene."

Like Winston Churchill addressing the people, Tom stood on the canteen table and boomed his voice as best he could to a slightly bemused and awkward crowd. With all the courage of an Amish resident at an electrical store, he began his impassioned speech.

"People of school, me and my friends here have been mocked and ridiculed by you for too long now." Tom felt the inspiration seep all through his body until he realised that from the looks of his fellow pupils, he was most likely only inspiring himself. Still, he persevered. "Why have you treated us like we are inferior? Is it because we are geeks? Is it because we are nerds or is it because we might be a little socially inept?"

"Nah mate, its cause your virgins," came a lone voice from the crowd.

That was it. The school canteen erupted into extroverted laughter. Tom's cheeks became blood red and he sheepishly climbed down from table. The day couldn't possibly get any worse. The boys had faced public humiliation before, many a time, but this was hitting a new high on the Richter scale.

"You gave it your best shot, buddy," Chilvers said.

Matt patted a hand on Tom's back. "I would have never have had the balls to do that."

"I just want people to notice us," Tom replied solemnly.

"One day, they will. Just not today, eh…"

Saving them from anymore embarrassment was the school bell. It was time for assembly. There at least, seated amongst their fellow pupils, they effortlessly faded into the crowd.

*

The auditorium slowly filled with the entire school body. Everybody was here to witness the latest offering from the drama department.

If standards were anything to go by from previous performances, however, then expectations were unanimously low. The students and faculty settled into their seats and wondered what distress they had caused in a previous life to deserve the torture of another early morning play. As the lights came down, many an audience member were already bored to tears and awaiting the sweet release of death.

The geeks took to their seats and frantically scanned the hall for any sight of their friend Mark. He had never missed a day of school in his life, so whatever the reason for his absence; it must be good.

Chilvers noted what play the drama club was showcasing this time, 'Romeo and Juliet'. He sighed, *Oh shit. I don't have it in me for this.*

The drama department hadn't had the most success when it came to shows of late. Last year their big summer production was *The Lion King.* It had been a bold and brave retelling of the classic Disney film but had ultimately been deemed 'utter bollocks' by the school newsletter and its twelve-year-old reviewer. The school, well known as the most deprived in the local area, had needed to cut some of its budget in order to save cash and spend it on more important things like heating and wage packets for the staff.

The drama department had been the first on the list to have their budget slashed and with it, the last of its dignity. *The Lion King* had featured a cast of five and no soundtrack due to copyright issues. The tiny lion cub of the story was played by a stray King Charles spaniel found on the field. The dog had become the star of the show by simply sitting stage left, then falling asleep, as if the tedious affair had become too much even for him. It didn't help that the lead drama teacher had cast himself as most of the ensemble background characters and spent the entire show parading around in nothing but an elephant mask and a piece of curtain.

Next, had come the shambolic Christmas production that was an original play entitled '*Jesus – The Truth of a Carpenter who worked with Wood*'.

It featured all the elements needed for a hit play but unfortunately the drama teacher behind the show was going through the early stages of a severe nervous breakdown and wrote the script himself. Whilst heavily medicated one night on a concoction of vodka and prescription pills, he wrote the play depicting Jesus Christ as an ageing homosexual who lived with his disciples and began an affair with his alcoholic step-father, Joseph.

The play had garnered a lot of attention from the local press and religious organisations. The head teacher, who had not seen the play himself beforehand, expressed his apologies and offered to personally make amends.

Instead, he sent some of the pupils to do community service for the elders of the church to save public face. Still, the mortified parents and guardians had called for the drama teacher in question to be fired. There was no need for the protests, however, as he was later found passed out naked on the field with a note wishing for whoever found him to take him to a psychiatric ward.

The geeks sat watching the latest offering of amateur theatre and their opinion was verging on abysmal. As they looked around, they noted that the students around them seemed to be drifting between various states of semi-consciousness and a full on coma.

Thankfully, to everyone's relief, the drama teacher was showcasing a semi-*Greatest Hits* version of Shakespeare's classic and they only had to stomach a few more famous scenes. This apparent act of kindness to save the students from boredom did not go unnoticed by the teaching faculty. The students, however, did not care in the slightest and impulsively took to their smartphones.

On the show went and with it, on came the aspiring actress portraying Juliet. The girl bore the title as head of the drama club, a title which was self-elected, and what she possessed in passion, she severely lacked in any considerable talent. "Romeo, Romeo, o' where for art thou now...my lover...thou....," she beautifully mangled.

Chilvers and Matt couldn't help but notice that she was standing on a cardboard erected balcony. While it wasn't out of the norm for school plays to use painted cardboard as scenery, it was strange to have their actors standing on them. However, what made this prop even more questionable was the fact that it had been built by little Huey, a hugely popular student who just happened to be blind.

Still, the ever-persistent Juliet ploughed on, awaiting the arrival of her Romeo.

Stage left and on entered the actor. His appearance sent bewildered whispers through the audience, not least for the geeks. There, in all his nerd glory, was their AWOL friend Mark.

"Did he tell you two about this?" Chilvers quipped.

Matt and Tom simply shook their heads.

Mark, with wiry dirty blonde hair and thick prescription glasses, looked the archetype of a small being in a strange land. With his arms and legs slightly out of proportion with his body, it only accentuated his bean shaped head.

And so he stood under the blinding spotlight, an odd looking boy with masses of perspiration seeping from him. Dressed in leftover rags from the previous plays, he looked every bit the court jester that he found himself unintentionally playing.

"I am standing underneath the balcony, my love... art thou," he amalgamated, ham acting hand gesture complete.

Matt buried his head in his hands. "He's going to commit social suicide."

"And bring us down with him," Tom piped in.

Juliet, undeterred by his lack of Shakespearean lingo, pressed on. "Whence did thou awaken the guards?"

"Eh?" was all Mark managed.

Chilvers wondered what possible gain Mark stood from being in the school play. He barely spoke a word in everyday circumstances and when he did it was only to be blunt and add his unique, if somewhat off-handed opinion on things. "What is he doing up there?"

Mark suddenly shifted his weight and dropped to one knee, then tilted his head to the audience to deliver his self-penned soliloquy. "I love this girl!" he boomed, his voice reverberating off the walls.

"Oh God," Chilvers grimaced. "There it is. Kill me now. End it! End it!"

"We have to stop him," came the voice of an anxious Tom.

On stage, Juliet couldn't hide her shock. "You what?" she hissed, suddenly realising she had broken character.

She then took the drastic choice to try and improvise her way out it, another actor's skill she tragically lacked. "You must save me whence, Romeo!"

"What?" Mark gawped. "Didn't you hear me? I said I love you! Don't you love me?"

Juliet realised that the whole school had become entranced by the bumbling reality show unfolding out in front of them. With her personal reputation at stake, in truth she was not respected at best, she flummoxed character completely to tell Mark how she really felt. "No! Now, piss off you little shit!"

Mark, not looking as wounded as one should after a public humiliation, simply shrugged. "Fine." And with that, he exited stage right.

Juliet was left alone.

As if the hopeful Oscar winner's morning couldn't get any worse, she felt the cardboard structure was about to give way. Her professionalism kept her in character. "Can someone hence save me from this rickety structure?"

No one did. Frankly, no one was bothered.

No one even tried apart from the drama teacher who was running wildly from the back, even if a little half-hearted. Juliet felt the set was going to give way.

Snap.

She felt it. "Oh-" was all she managed before she went hurtling to the floor in spectacular fashion.

In the wings, Mark simply smirked. "She'll need mouth to mouth," he chimed, his tongue smacking heavily on his lips as he prepared for his first kiss. Albeit an unreciprocated one.

*

Deep in the woodland area, not too far from the school, a rondure wonderment lay in a heap.

Its exterior was charred and the flames engulfing it rapidly began to spread the whole outer casing of reflective metal. The heap was modest in size and while it bore little resemblance to anything on earth, someone may have simply took it out for scrap.

The only puzzlement, if there was one, and if a passer-by had cast witness, was a strange appearance from the smoke and flames. Anyone looking in might have described the vision before them as a small hand.

A small hand that just happened to be blue.

CHAPTER TWO

Dejected. That is the only word that epitomized how the boys felt. They physically couldn't muster any other emotion from their cortex. After the disaster that had been the school play, AKA: Mark's declaration of love, they found themselves once again banished to the decomposing bench in the far reaches of the playground.

The bell had rung to herald the mid-morning break and this was a time that Chilvers loathed as much as anything. In truth, he positively seethed at the very idea of it.

It was here on the playground that any outsider could easily distinguish the social hierarchy from the kaleidoscope of bodies before them.

At the centre of attention were the footballers. They kicked around the ball with an edge of competitiveness every chance they got, mainly to keep in shape but more notably to impress the girls who were always casting a sly eye. It was these girls that made up the bulk of the playground activity, that is unless it was raining, and then they could be found applying heaps of cement worthy make-up to their zit-lined faces and they were always discussing their next sleep over, and more importantly, who and who not should be invited.

Next down the order of command stood the teacher's pet; while it was cringe worthy to watch them weasel their way around their favourite teachers with puke inducing remarks, one had to keep them close, as one bad word from one of these prickly students and you could find yourself in the teacher's bad books.

In the farthest corner possibly from any social group sat the geeks.

Quiet. Unassuming. Alone.

Each of them produced a sandwich from their backpacks and in turn pondered the thought that one day their mothers would not be around to make their lunches for them. Hauntingly, they knew that one day they would have to do it themselves. They shuddered at the very trauma of it.

A calm moment of silence fell among the group. This was sometimes the case with the boys but they were always comfortable enough in each other's company not to feel the need to make small talk. They were close enough friends for it not to feel awkward in silence; more often than not, anyway, they all knew what the other was thinking.

Eventually though, curiosity got the better of Tom. "Mark, I have to ask...what the hell were you thinking?"

Mark looked up, not the slightest hint of emotion portrayed on his chubby face. "I thought it was a good idea at the time."

Tom rolled his eyes. "How could you possibly think that that was a good idea?"

"Do I dare need to remind you about last Christmas?" Mark retorted.

What Mark was referring to was one of the more traumatic events in their many, many misadventures.

The latest *Star Wars* film was due to be released shortly before Christmas and so Tom had taken it upon himself to announce that all of the group should camp out in front of the cinema a few days before to guarantee the best seats.

While everyone else had pointed out that in the age of internet magic, you could simply pre-book your seats and arrive ten minutes before the film started, Tom viscously protested, saying that it was how the American movie-going public used to watch their films. He also said it would add more experience to a huge event in their young lives.

The other three finally agreed, albeit a little reluctantly, and concluded that camping out three nights before was justified. Tom contacted the local press stating that if they wanted an exclusive interview with the boys, then they would have to pay. Once again, the other boys were dumfounded by Tom's thirst for fame. The events that transpired were nothing short of a living nightmare.

Firstly, and most obviously, came the ridicule. Boy racers had spotted the boys camping out, they then decided to come back a few hours later armed with bags of dog shit, or at least the boys hoped it was dog shit, and subsequently hurled it at the boys.

Despite the smell, the boys refused to budge.

The following night saw the attack of an abnormally sized badger, which had smelt the boy's supplies of peanut butter sandwiches. The badger clawed at their flabby bodies and left each of them with lifelong scars.

Despite their bodies being ravaged, the boys refused to budge.

On the last night, the one of the film's premier, the boys were now mere hours away from the historic midnight screening of the new film. None of them, however, had been prepared for the severe drop in temperature.

And so, only minutes away from midnight, the geeks found themselves rushed to A&E with possible frostbite and suspected hypothermia.

A few days later when they returned home, a flash of good fortune finally rained down upon them. The cinema's manager had heard about the boy's mishaps, so he decided to send them free complimentary tickets to a special Christmas Eve showing.

The boys couldn't believe their luck and energetically geared up to complete their conquest and face the harrowing winter.

Mark had, for some unknown reason, been left in charge of the tickets, in hindsight; it was doomed from the start. He somehow managed to place the tickets in a charity gift box that his mother sent to third world countries as part of her volunteer work with the church.

With no tickets and nothing but empty hands, the boys trudged through wind and rain to the Christmas Eve showing. This happened to be an IMAX 3D screening, so the boys were left broke for the remainder of the Christmas holidays.

Meanwhile, some poor African orphan opened up a box, hoping to find food but was left riddled with confusion at the discovery of four ticket stubs.

Tom simply shrugged off the incident. "We made it into the local paper didn't we? Not all bad news if I say so myself."

Chilvers waved his hand, as if to throw the conversation away. "Look, none of that matters now. What does matter is if Mark really liked this girl."

"I don't know really," he replied. "I don't think so. Some good did come of it though."

"How can you possibly reach that conclusion?" Matt demanded. "The poor girl has broken bones in eight places. She had to be carried out the school on a stretcher."

Mark grinned manically. "I got to kiss her, didn't I?"

"That wasn't a kiss. Your demonically possessed tongue was aiming for her mouth but missed. You savaged that poor girl's half-glazed eyeball with your tongue!"

"It still counts. It was physical contact."

"Well, that's true. I have to give you that one."

The four boys fell into a trance, lost in thought dreaming about members of the opposite sex, wondering if their time would ever come.

Suddenly, Tom leapt up from the bench, and then inhaled a vast amount of oxygen. The others knew he was about to launch into one of his epic speeches. They braced themselves.

"People, people, people," he began. "This talk of women is getting tiresome. Why keep pondering that of which we know we will never have? Like historians on the quest for the Holy Grail, ultimately, they are always left disappointed. We on the other hand, are chasing a different kind of end game. And now my friends; it is finally in our grasp."

"What the hell are you talking about?"

Tom reached down to his bag and produced a small box. "This!"

"It's a box."

"Yes, I know it's a box but it's what's inside the box that's of great importance to us."

The others rolled their eyes. They had seen all of this before. Tom, apparently assuming the role of a magician's assistant, theatrically revealed the contents of the box.

"It's a…tie," Chilvers remarked.

"Yes, I know it's a bloody tie but this is no ordinary tie. This tie…was once worn…by Harrison Ford."

"Sweet Baby Jesus!"

"I don't believe it!"

"Fuck me!"

Tom caressed the tie like an emotional groom might hold his bride to be. "I know, I know, it is the most beautiful thing I have ever seen. You don't want to know how much I paid for it."

The others were awed. To think that this piece of garment had been in the presence of their hero was simply the stuff of dreams! Chilvers went to reach for the hallowed item but Tom pulled it away. "I need to touch it. I just want to smell it," Chilvers cried out.

"In time, all of us can take hold of this piece of gold dust."

Matt pulled out a pen and pad. "I suggest we devise a rota. Distribute the time of the tie evenly so we all get a fair share of it."

"Not a bad idea," Mark quipped. "This is the greatest day of my life," he added.

Their shared sense of euphoria was about to come to a screeching halt. Matt spotted them first, and then quickly alerted the rest of the group.

Tom meticulously placed the tie back in its box then safely placed it into his bag. Chilvers sat up to face the rest of the group. "If this goes wrong, sacrifice each other. Save the tie. No matter what."

"Agreed," came the unanimous reply. They all slowly picked up their belongings in the hope of making a quick escape.

Alas, all their escape routes were blocked.

"Where is all you bitches running off to so quickly?"

Chilvers winced, not in physical pain but for the emotional scarring that was about to come. "We're not looking for trouble. We're just heading off to class."

Rigger simply cocked his head to one side, while an arrogant smirk formed across his face. "Well, with attitude like that, I would say that all you's have found trouble."

Matt grunted. He had become accustomed to this ritualistic bullying but he still couldn't stand to listen to this god awful grammar. "Please, leave us alone."

The plea fell on deaf ears.

Rigger was a year older than the geeks and no matter where he went he was always accompanied by his fellow tormenter, Burnsey.

No one in school ever dared to call them by the real names; Michael and Benjamin. (Apparently these names weren't deemed 'street' enough by the hard men) Their days consisted of bunking off classes, terrorizing the younger kids and trying to score tallies with the girls.

They conducted themselves, like all bullies do, with an air of self-importance and with a mild hint of insecurity. Chilvers picked up on it and they knew it. On weekends when the geeks were unfortunate enough to run into the pair, they noted how they wore far too much jewellery and seemed to get drunk off just one can of cider in the park.

Tom had always presumed that they were trying to emulate the Kray Twins, walking with a certain swagger. Tom liked to put it a different way; "they walk like need a damn good shit," was one of his favourite sayings.

Chilvers bravely summoned his shoulders to broaden. "We'd like to go now."

"No chance," Rigger proclaimed.

Burnsey snapped his fingers. "Pay up, now. All of you's! Four quid each."

The demoralisation never got any easier. Rigger and Burnsey always drew attention to themselves wherever they went and today was no exception. While the boys fumbled in their pockets for some loose change, they noticed that a little crowd had gathered around.

They were offered a brief moment of reprieve though, as Chilvers spotted the appearance of two girls; Emily and Shaquan.

These two merchants of gossip spread a feeling of dread wherever they stepped foot. They would casually hover by any student that was locked in conversation, closely listening in for a titbit of information about someone that they could then use to their malicious advantage.

The girls did whatever they had to in order to assert themselves as the Queen Bees of school life. However, like even the mightiest of warriors, the girls had a weakness; they were helplessly in love with Rigger and Burnsey.

While the pair of would-be-hard men didn't mind the attention of the ladies, they liked to keep them at a distance, retaining their lone wolf images. As the two girls approached, worthy of a witches coven, it was painfully obvious that they would do anything to win the love of the pair of bullies.

Chilvers didn't want any more drama than was already unfolding. "Please, this is between us and them. Not you," he pleaded with the girls.

Emily stepped back. "Oh no, you do not disrespect us like that, you little fucking nerd."

Shaquan pursed her lips. "That is no way to talk to a mother of two! Do not come up in my face speaking that shit!"

Tom jerked his head. "Wait, wait…you're a mother of two?"

"Got a problem with that bitch? I hope you ain't got no problem otherwise our boys here is gonna destroy you."

"Since when have you been a mother? Aren't you a little young?

"Is fourteen too young? That's racism if I ever saw it?

"How is that racist? I was referring to your age."

"Oooh, now who's chatting shit you little freak? When my son, Anthony Declan, grows up, all you geeks is gonna be working for him, yeah!"

"Wait a second…you called your kid…Ant and Dec?"

"Problem, bitch?"

"No, no. I like Ant and Dec, just not too sure that they would approve of their names being used on a little shit like yours."

A speechless Shaquan glared at Tom. "You know that shit did not just come from your mouth."

In a surprising turn of events, the boys were not beaten up by their usual enemies of Rigger and Burnsey but instead they were forced to defend themselves from the school's gossip lovers.

Emily used her false nails to scratch the geeks, clawing at their eyes like a wild cat defending itself. Rigger and Burnsey took a step back, finding the whole situation impossibly hilarious. They were forced to intervene, however, when Shaquan picked up a huge rock and with surprising strength, hurled it at Tom.

"Easy, easy," Rigger cried out. "Everybody just chill, yeah?"

Tom was having none of it. He was seeing red. He reached for his bag, pulling out the beloved Harrison Ford tie.

"No, Tom, don't do it!" Matt gasped. "Think of the tie!"

It was too late. Tom wrapped the tie around each hand and launched himself towards Rigger. With immense force that surprised even himself, Tom jumped up on Rigger's back, pulling the tie over his neck.

Emily began to palpitate hysterically. "That little nerd is gonna kill my man! Somebody stop him!"

"Burnsey, baby, get them geeks! Cut their eyes out!" Shaquan screeched.

Right on cue, the crowd instantly dispersed.

The sight that greeted the headmaster did not please him one bit. "Gentlemen, my office, now!"

Tom fell to the ground while Rigger was quick to amplify his injuries, seemingly having difficulty breathing. Chilvers was first to put his hand up. "Sir, I know what it looks like but believe me, you have the wrong end of the stick."

"There is no wrong end of a stick, young man. There are just two ends of a stick. Do not patronize me."

"It was all them geeks, sir! They've gone mad. They say it's the quiet ones you should always look for," came Emily's defence for Rigger.

"You know that shit, sir!" Shaquan chipped in.

"Don't swear at me young girl," came the monotone reply of the head master. "I want all of you in my office, immediately."

"But…"

"Just get to my office."

Rigger and Burnsey headed off immediately. They had been disciplined many times before; quite frankly it no longer bothered them what went on their record. They knew the geeks would be a different matter entirely, so as they walked off, they turned around to give the boys a smug grin.

Burnsey even winked at them.

Chilvers, mortified at the destination he was heading, felt a swelling of anger in his stomach. "Well, thanks a lot Tom," came his sarcastic droll. "My reputation is tarnished. What will my parents say?"

"Why did you even attack him?" Matt quizzed. "We're the victims here, we don't get into fights. That's not who we are. You've excelled yourself, Tom, you really have."

Mark, clearly thinking something polar opposite, positively beamed as the strolled to the headmaster's office. "I think this will do wonders for our street cred."

"You see," Tom said. "Someone's looking on the bright side of this."

"Don't, Tom," Chilvers barked. "I think you've done enough damage for one day."

*

The Las Vegas Strip, Nevada

Hank settled into his room overlooking the world famous *Caesar's Palace*. He took in the view of it before promptly closing the drapes.

He wasn't here for that. In fact, he wasn't here for any of the famous dealings in America's so called sin city. Hank wasn't bothered about the gambling, drinking or seeing any of the shows. He was here to work. He was here to fulfil a lifetime ambition.

Ever since he was a child, Hank had been fascinated by space but more specifically he loved aliens. He was obsessed with life from another planet, mainly, as he was secretly convinced that the time was nearing when the world as we knew it would crumble and modern civilisation would be forced to welcome a new race of higher intelligent beings to take control. Thus the people of earth would enter a new world order.

He knew his passion and as God as his witness, he was going to see it through.

Over the past decade, Hank had poured over every available material concerning Area 51. He was well aware of most of the conspiracy theories associated with it. There were reports on dozens of projects going on inside the compound. Things like secret weather machines, futuristic technology that would equip soldiers with chameleon like camouflage and then, of course, there were the hybrid beings conspiracies. All mouth-watering. All deeply fascinating.

None of these were of importance to Hank though; he was here for one thing only, the world famous alien that had crashed in Roswell in 1947.

The theories were wild; the stories documented on the subject ran high into thousands but was mostly debunked as wild fantasy by conspiracy theorists.

He had told his family that he was taking a vacation to Vegas as a cover story but in reality, he was here to complete his mission; break into Area 51 and reveal the truth to the world. The notion of actually entering Area 51 was the trickiest part. He had no idea how he was going to do it.

At the back of his mind, a tiny voice told him it was ridiculous but so many other voices in his head told him he was right.

As Hank sat there in his hotel suite, reading book after book, he hoped one day that he would be proven right. He ordered himself room service and flicked on the T.V.

News channels were once again echoing the same stories of modern day life; more violence somewhere, another tragedy somewhere else, more warnings about terror somewhere else.

Hank longed for change.

Little did he know that change was about to come.

CHAPTER THREE

"Boys, boys, boys...all this was over a tie?"

The four geeks solemnly looked to the floor, like prisoners awaiting execution on death row. They had never been in the head master's office before and they did not like it one bit.

They had desperately tried to explain their version of events but it didn't help the fact that Rigger was the headmaster's son. If Riggers performance didn't improve, he was almost certainly not going to get into a decent college or any college for that matter. The odds were stacked against them but they tried one last ditch attempt to reclaim their pride.

Chilvers stepped forward from the line, now feeling like he was a lawyer about to give an articulate defence for his client. "Sir, if I may. This was really just a huge misunderstanding. While it's true that we don't see eye to eye with your son, it was a joke that got a little out of hand."

The headmaster contemplated this. "I see," he murmured, rubbing his chin. "But that still doesn't rectify the situation. I did, after all, see young Thomas here strangling my son with a tie."

Tom waved his hand to protest. "I have to say that we are losing sight of the bigger picture here. That valuable tie of mine is no longer in mint condition due to the incident. I suggest that Rigger or yourself foot the bill."

"I beg your pardon, young man!"

"He's a little confused, sir," Matt stammered. "What he means to say is that we are very sorry indeed for any trouble caused."

"No, no, please Thomas, continue. I am very interested in your line of thought." The tone of the headmaster was far more snake-like than the boys would have liked.

"Well, sir," Tom beamed, nothing standing in his way. "The tie once belonged to one Mr. Harrison Ford. The value of it to us is indescribable."

"Young man," the head master interjected. "Do you hear yourself? What on earth has gotten into you?"

"Very simple, sir," Tom stated. "What has gotten into me is unquestionable, unequivocal fanaticism. Nothing, I mean, nothing, can take that away from us."

The boys lowered their heads once more. Tom spoke with reason and some semblance of logic but it was obvious that the head master didn't want to hear it.

"Right," the headmaster began. "I have decided what course of action I shall take. I have no doubt that some of the blame must fall on my son. I will deal with him in due course. As for you boys, I cannot let violence like this slide. In light of your impeccable history until now, I shall award you with a mild suspension. In other words, you will be suspended for the rest of the day. Go home, do homework…no, wait, go outside! Get some sunshine; heaven knows you look like you need it. I'd say that that is a fair deal all round, don't you? Good day, gentlemen."

Chilvers wasn't overly impressed. His mind raced at the thought of having a black mark against his name but there was really nothing he could do. He reluctantly nodded his head in agreement, as did Matt and Mark. Tom however, was clearly thinking on a different wave length as he aggressively directed a finger at the headmaster.

"You shit," were the two words that leapt with venom from his mouth.

"Your suspension is now a week and that goes for all of you," the headmaster quipped.

Chilvers, ever the diplomat, stepped up to the post. "Sir, please, Tom's very upset, we all are. We don't want to make things worse. We'll be leaving now."

"Can we at least have the tie back," Tom pleaded.

"Good Lord, no," came the curt reply. "I've been doing some digging on this little beauty and it turns out that it's worth quite a small fortune. Thus, I am confiscating it."

"Oh, the audacity! You mean you're going to sell our tie!"

"Absolutely."

"You c-"

Before Tom could seal their fates to expulsion, the other boys removed him from the headmaster's office as quickly as was humanly possible.

*

Soho, New York City.

Liam Walker stared down his refection in the mirror. He casually applied his aftershave, secretly cursing himself for using it, not wanting to waste it as it had cost three hundred dollars. Still, it was all part of his pulling image.

He was twenty-eight years old, with a solid head of hair for his age and an athletic build that most men would be envious of. His suit had cost him upwards of two thousand dollars, something which he had recently started using as his chat-up line. It impressed the girls, money always did.

By twenty-six, Liam had been named as Vice President of the graphic design company where he had interned for nine years previously. He had a great group of friends; had near enough travelled the world once over and now found himself stone cold sober in his apartment with a beautiful girl at four o'clock in the morning.

Liam often hit the swanky bars and clubs that Soho had to offer but lately he'd been venturing to these watering holes on a work night. The obscure fact about these bar visits was that he didn't drink. Liam always ordered a diet lemonade soda with ice and if anyone asked what he was drinking, he'd tell them it was a G&T. He'd stopped drinking a few months ago in order to keep his physic on top form.

So, here he was, ready to perform the mating ritual. He walked into his living room to find his one-night stand lying semi-naked on the couch. She was stunning in every way possible, her eyes glowed like candles in the dark and her slim figure was only accentuated by the moonlight.

He couldn't for the life of him remember her name but that fell by the wayside as she slowly rose up to walk towards him.

She kissed him, he kissed her back.

They stayed locked in a motoring mouth movement for a while as they stumbled around his apartment. He thought he was leading her to his bedroom but his judgment was off with all the excitement. They ended up in his spare bedroom that had been converted into his man cave.

"You didn't tell me you had a kid," she slurred, alcohol continuing to intoxicate her system.

"I…err…don't, this is my stuff," Liam stammered out.

Her face dropped. "This is all yours?" She nervously eyed his man-den taking in the landscape of toys before her. "You collect kid's toys?" her tone sounding less playful by the second.

"They're not toys, they're collectables."

"But…I didn't have you pegged as one of those…weird folk." She seemed to grow sober almost instantaneously and the irresistible atmosphere from moments ago now seemed eons away.

Liam didn't take the insult kindly. "You know what; I think this date is over. I'll show you out."

"No, no, no, I'm sorry. I didn't mean to offend you. Show me something. Honest. I won't laugh."

Liam hesitated. His collection of memorabilia was deeply personal to him, in some ways it was an extension of who he was, another lost soul trying to find his voice in a world filled with so many. Liam was simply another face in the crowd trying to bring a little bit of joy in his life.

With great reluctance, he picked up a statue. "This is one of the first items I ever got; a few years ago I was able to get it signed by Mark Hamill." His face shone with gleeful disposition.

His date so desperately tried to hide her laughter, although it now no longer came across as slightly playful, instead it verged on mockery.

Stung with a pang of pain, Liam showed his date to the front door and bid her farewell.

He made himself a coffee then settled in his chair awaiting the arrival of sunrise. He flicked through his phone checking social media. He became dismayed when he noticed some friends of his had become first time parents during the night and he groaned at other friends who seemed forever locked in a state of gaiety.

As he felt his eyes become heavy, his phone vibrated. An old university friend from England had sent him a brief video recording from a few hours ago.

From what Liam could make out, the footage seemed to show a UFO cascading through the sky. He'd seen footage like this before but even Liam had to admit there was something different about this one.

Something tangible. Something beautiful.

*

It was approaching mid-day when the geeks embarked upwards into the woods. The sun's rays were beating down with intense exuberance while an apathetic silence hovered over the group.

The others noted that at least Tom seemed to be feeling some kind of remorse following his shambolic behaviour in the headmaster's office.

These four sufferers of the human condition trekked alongside the glistening river, not enjoying a moment of it. The four friends had rarely fought in the approximately decade long friendship, a pact that had been cemented in a classroom a lifetime ago.

The geeks, then just a tender aged five, had been thrown together in a new class after a shortage of teaching staff. To ease the pupils into their environment, the teacher had encouraged a show-and-tell on the first morning. She urged each of them to summon up a little presentation, declaring that it was a good way to gage their articulacy and to help the more veiled students to overcome their shyness.

A majority of the boys had brought in footballs or their home team's strip while the girls showed off posters or CD's of their favourite boy band.

To the delight of the teacher, one student had shown off an encyclopaedia which she was working her way through. To her dismay, however, came the sight of one pupil producing his parent's divorce documents and then announcing that he was going to burn them in the schoolyard.

Next, a bright eyed Matt, who displayed a show-business like attitude towards public speaking, stood up in front of his peers. From his pocket he pulled out a *Darth Vader* action figure. He continued to describe in immense detail the history of the character, its importance in a film and how the toy had been his favourite birthday present from a few weeks ago.

Tom rose next to talk about his show-and-tell item; also a *Darth Vader* action figure. Matt listened closely as this boy before him spoke a little differently about his toy. Instead of re-enacting the films, the young Tom proceeded to explain how he wanted to make an action figure version of himself, much to the amusement of his teacher.

Thirdly, Mark took to the floor to proclaim he had also brought *Darth Vader* toy as well. Just as the sweet little Mark was about to launch into his tirade about his toy, the teacher pointed out that Mark was actually holding a *Princess Leia* action figure.

Mark then continued to improvise a new presentation and discussed how milk was produced by the female member of the species, even using the toy as a model. To conclude; and to the horror of his teacher, Mark accounted vivid memories of being breastfed as an infant.

Finally, it was the turn of Chilvers. Even at the age of five, he stood shoulders above the rest of his classmates. He didn't speak, though; instead he showed the class his *Darth Vader* figure, then smiled at his fellow future geeks.

They smiled back, thus forever sealing the fate of their friendship.

Those days of care-free innocence were now fiercely scorched into their memories.

Chilvers often looked back on those breath-taking days with a warming of his heart as he was reminded of a time when he was truly happy. He often remarked at how there was no greater feeling in the world than that as a child of when they believed in Santa Claus.

These days, however, he wanted nothing more than to go back and find that feeling. Those moments were now lost in time, transcending into feelings of nostalgia and now those memories were nothing more than a brush stroke on his canvas of life.

Chilvers didn't like the innate feeling that he was already living in the shadows of glory days. The poignancy of his reflection weighed deeply on his soul as a profound sadness mercilessly inched towards his heart.

He despised these feelings, so he physical jolted his body to try and rid them.

Chilvers abruptly halted in front of the group and then turned to address them. "This is not us," he boomed. "First of all, Tom, you were clearly in the wrong for your actions today in the headmaster's office and on the playground. I hope you fully realise the consequences of your actions, not just for yourself but for your comrades here."

Chilvers didn't give him time to respond; instead he pursued his trail of thought with such velocity that it startled the remainder of the group.

"Tom, you made a mistake but that's what people do. Our job as your friends is to now let go of that and put it behind us. You need to think before you open your mouth; if you do that, we might just avoid circumstances like this in the future.

"Now, I know that each of us has a justified amount of anxiety at the prospect of telling our parents about how we are fugitives of the school for the rest of the week, but I assure you that we will face each parent in turn and with each other, because that's what friends do, they face life together. They rejoice in the good and stand together in the bad.

"Quite simply, we will be there for each other. If you hurt, I hurt. If you need help, I'll be there before you hang up the phone. We will act selflessly and we will try to do the right thing. We're loving people, I know that, and sometimes, just sometimes, we might get it right."

Chilvers felt a wave of relief wash over him, as well as the rising of a small lump in his throat. The boys, like most teenagers, very rarely spoke about their inner most feelings but Chilvers had felt that the end justified the means. He noticed, too, that his friends seemed to acknowledge the sentiment.

Matt and Mark smiled in unison and then patted Chilvers on the shoulder. "Agreed."

Tom smiled and then offered a subtle nod.

The beauty of male friendship was the fact it didn't need to be overstated.

"What next?" Matt shrugged.

Tom leaned forward, his confidence slowly coming to the surface now that the drama was behind them. "Well, we are still in a state of mourning. I still have the packaging that the Harrison Ford tie came in. We could hold a memorial."

"Put it away," Mark wailed. "The memory is too painful."

"Well, I say that we give it a funeral a proper funeral. Lord knows that this day needs some kind of optimism," Chilvers concurred. "Now, I say that we bury this box in proper fashion. The Harrison Ford tie brought us a brief, fleeting moment of happiness. Does anybody want to say a few words?"

Mark couldn't hold back the tears. "I can't. I'm too weak."

Tom usurped his voice to slowly begin to sing *Coldplay's Fix You*. Thankfully, before he butchered the song completely, Matt stepped forward to say a few words.

Matt cleared his throat. "Right, this tie may have just have been a tie to some, even to the bearer, Mr. Harrison Ford, it was probably just a tie but to us, it was something so much more.

"Never again shall we find ourselves in the presence of our hero but we shall be in the forever gratitude of this humble piece of fabric. Ashes to ashes, dust to dust. Rest in peace, Harrison Ford tie."

The other boys saluted the box as Matt placed it gently in the stream.

Mark began to hum the funeral march as it drifted slowly down the stream towards the esotery of forgotten time.

A few moments of silence ensued.

Then, suddenly, a deafening explosion of volcano-like magnitude erupted behind them. The tranquil atmosphere was then thrown into earth shattering cracks.

The boys were rapidly hurled to the floor as thunderous booms conically cocooned into the sky. The boys hit the ground with a painful thud and their surrounding became a blur as the moment of terror came to a deafening end.

The geeks stayed bolted to the floor, fear coursing through their veins as shock poured into their hearts.

A few minutes past, allowing Chilvers to cautiously get to his feet. "What the hell?" he whispered.

He looked down to the other three who slowly rose to their feet. They finally allowed their eyes to gaze on the vision before them. Through the trees and smoke lay something that they could make out in the clear daylight.

There was no denying it.

"Dear God."

"I don't believe it."

"It's a..."

"It's a spaceship," Matt stated, unable to manage anything else. "It's a fucking spaceship."

"Or it could be gypsies," offered Mark. Having watched a few documentaries on gypsies, he considered himself quite the expert on the folk.

"Fucking gypsies!"

"Well, it's more logical than a spaceship."

"That is most definitely a spaceship," Tom urged.

"What should we do?" asked Matt.

"Nothing."

"I like the sound of that."

"Could be terrorists?"

"Or the government?"

"Or a practical joke?"

"A reality T.V show?"

"I like the sound of the latter," squawked Mark, teeth beginning to chatter with fear.

"Perhaps it's a prop for a film?" Tom put forward.

Not a bad idea, Chilvers thought. He felt himself relaxing a bit. He took a breath. "Who wants to do what?"

Matt craned his neck. "I say we go in and have a look but I'm not going first."

"Me neither," Chilvers abruptly pointed out.

"You guys aren't thinking big enough, you're not thinking grand enough," Tom yelled. "What if this isn't a film or TV prop? What if this is something very special indeed? What if we are the ones to find it?"

"It all seems a little bit too coincidental if you ask me," Matt pondered.

"Maybe it's no coincidence, but fate…" The words left Tom's mouth ever so slowly.

Chilvers offered a wry smile. "Tom, I do love you, but you're a dreamer. A hopeless dreamer."

"I'm a dreamer who still believes," Tom shot back, a fierce fire burning in his eyes.

"Are we decided that we are going to have a look," Matt asked.

"Yes," Tom excitably replied. "But who's going first?"

"Not me."

"Not me."

"Not me."

That left one person.

Chilvers turned to Mark, who by this point had lost all colour from his face. Chilvers bent down to Mark's height and offered him a friendly pat on the shoulder before adding some words of wisdom.

"Aliens...very dangerous...*you go first.*"

Chilvers couldn't help but laugh at his own joke. He decided that inspecting this heap of flaming metal would kill some time and could be a fun memory in a few months from now, something that he and his friends could look back on.

Mark felt himself be sick in his mouth but he didn't let it show. There was no point protesting. It was an unwritten rule that one should never back down in the face of danger. He swallowed hard but all he could taste was sick, reminding him of everything that his mother had ever cooked. *Rancid stuff.*

He turned and looked at the savaged piece of wreckage before him. "Here, I go."

The shortest and podgiest member of the group slowly waddled forward. The other boys watched in disbelief as this normally cowardly teenager stepped into the darkened entrance of the ship.

They swallowed hard as he slowly disappeared from view. Chilvers wondered if this was a good idea on second thought, but he was still an advocate of the practical joke theory.

One second passed.

Five seconds passed.

Twenty seconds passed until finally they heard a fumbling noise.

"*Can someone throw me a torch,*" the voice from inside cried.

Everyone let out their collective breaths.

"Mark," Matt yelled. "What can you see?"

"Fuck all, that's why I need a torch."

"It's not something we tend to carry about with us," Tom interjected. "Can't you use the light of your phone?"

"Suppose so," Mark yelled back, still lost in the void of the ship.

Chilvers saw a little light flicker from inside the entrance way but this was quickly followed by darkness and a thud.

"Shit."

"Mark, what's happened?" Chilvers anxiously cried.

"I've dropped my phone. It's okay. I'll feel my way around."

"God help us," Matt sighed, as he looked to an evermore worried Chilvers.

"Yes," came the cry of the intrepid explorer. *"I think I've found the control centre!"*

"How do you know that if you can't see anything," Tom stated. He turned to Chilvers. "I have a feeling that this is not going to end well."

"I've found a bit of light. I think it's okay to come in."

The boys all looked at each other. If Mark had been brave enough to go in, then surely they must. They set their watches to glow-in-the-dark-mode and walked up to the opening hatch way of the ship.

"Gentlemen," Chilvers said. "It's been a pleasure."

Tom seemed not to hear Chilvers or feel Matt's hand on his back; for he was lost in his own world. His eyes lit up like a child on Christmas morning as he surveyed the spaceship from every conceivable angle. "You know, this would make an awesome toy," he whispered softly.

And with that, they entered the heap of metal.

With all four boys now inside a passageway of the spaceship, they were blindly thumbing their way around in the pitch black darkness. The only ignition of light came from Tom's glow-in-the-dark watch.

Tom noted, from what he could barely make out, at just how battered the interior of the silver object seemed to be.

None of them could see each other, but they all bore terrified expressions on their faces as they tentatively walked through the corridors of the ship.

"I wish my father could see this, he would have loved it," Tom whispered.

Matt did a double take. "Wait," he pressed. "Has your father passed away?"

"No. He's at work."

They continued to tip-toe through the blackened hallway and wondered just what was waiting for them in the inner sanctum of their new found venture.

"Whatever this thing is," Chilvers thought aloud. "It took a severe beating."

"Looks like my nan drove it," Mark said, trying to inject some humour into an otherwise tense situation. He instantly felt a tiny bit bad for the comment on his Nan and for her accident in unknowingly reversing over a small child. It hadn't helped her case that the police had deduced that she had failed the standardized breathalyser test. It also didn't help the fact that her defence was, in her words, a once in a lifetime opportunity; she had categorically stated that it was okay if the child had been run over because she had been craning her neck as she thought she had seen Cliff Richard coming out of Tesco.

Tom broke off ahead a few steps and turned back to the group.

Still keeping his voice low, he shook his head disbelief. "To think," he began. "To think, that this could actually be an alien ship! I think it is! And I know that you all think it is, too! Stop pretending like the rest of you haven't made your minds up already."

Chilvers suddenly felt his stomach turn in a thousand directions. He aged fifty years in mere moments. *How could he be so stupid?*

His mouth went dry. His eyes ached and his knees almost buckled from beneath him. They had let their excitement get the better of them. But now it was over. In the dim light, he looked each of his friends in the eye.

"If this is an alien ship...then where are the aliens?"

PART II:

BLUE BEINGS

CHAPTER FOUR

"If this is an alien ship...then where are the aliens?"

FIFTY THREE MINUTES EARLIER...

The heap of metal lay burning in the middle of the woodland, engulfed in flames and smoke. The possibility of it exploding any minute was probably high. Its entry to earth had been unquestionably loud and no doubt local neighbours would have alerted the emergency services, worried of what the noise might be.

For the passengers of the heap of metal, it was now or never.

From the view port window of the ship emerged a tiny, blue, alien hand, followed by another, then a third, and finally a fourth. The hands then hoisted up small blue bodies through the windows and their tiny eyes squinted and scanned their unfamiliar, yet distinctive surroundings.

So, there it was: an alien arrival on earth.

And nobody was around to see it.

What people may have seen, though, had they been around, was a blue blur whipping through the forest with accelerating speed.

*

FOURTEEN MINUTES LATER ...

Every town has a road where the majority of the residents would love to live.

Prinston Way was no exception.

The sun seemed to set there like something out of a classic feel-good American comedy. The children who grew up on the street all moved to go on and succeed in whatever their aspiring hearts desired.

The elders who resided there always looked like they lived into their early nineties and could always be found enjoying their retirement with afternoon naps and long reading sessions, sometimes they even summoned the energy to go and get a paper.

It was idyllic in every way possible. It was the envy of other neighbourhoods.

On the street lay one house in particular that exuberated warmth from every window imaginable.

It was the home of Geraldine and David. In a street where everyone knew everyone and everyone in turn seemed to be either classed as an 'Aunty' or 'Uncle', it was common knowledge that Geraldine and David were the most likeable couple in the neighbourhood.

David, now in his late eighties, had rightfully earned the title of the 'Street Clown' with his dead on impressions of everyone who lived close by and his rapid fire deliveries at BBQ's.

David was a former banker who had held onto his working class morals and magical sense of humour. Though he wore a shirt and tie, he was a blue collar at heart. After retiring from the firm only a few months ago, he was now enjoying his days with his model trains and with his newly found joy of the walking club.

Geraldine, his wife of thirty-four years, was an American gal through and through. She had travelled to England after meeting David not long after the war. Despite being seventy-nine, the lady from the Deep South had aged gracefully, and still carried a song in her heart, no matter what the time of day. The values of her ancestry transcended into her now very British way of life.

If you needed a couple to mind your kids, they were the couple.

If you needed help arranging a charity function, they were ones whose door you knocked.

If you needed a shoulder, then you would run to them.

There was one reason in particular that people loved dropping by the couple's house; Geraldine's cooking.

The smells that came from the kitchen had people talking for days. One local paper has described one of Geraldine's cheesecakes as '...*simply orgasmic and better than a Sunday night with my wife*!' much to the controversy of the local town.

Geraldine was always cooking and today was no exception.

The American southerner stood with a knife in one hand and cheese grater in the other. She blissfully hummed away as she opened the oven door and busily worked her hard-grafted fingers to their core. With cookies cooling off on the shelf, Geraldine pulled out her quiche and took a long whiff of her pie.

"Smells good," she beamed, smiling to herself.

She turned and called out down the hallway. "David, suppers done, come get it before the neighbours do!" Though she spoke with a tinge of coyness, she secretly loved how popular her food was.

The sun was shining for once and Geraldine had opened the door and windows. She turned the radio up which was blasting some Country and Western of old, reminding her of her own glorious sun-baked childhood.

As if on cue and abruptly out of nowhere, a vicious gust of wind blew right through the kitchen.

"Damn, weather," she grumbled. "I'll be damned by the Lord Himself if I ever get used to y'all climate."

Geraldine hobbled over to the door and closed it shut. While the airwaves were filled with cut-loose honkytonks of her homeland, Geraldine missed the tiny pitter-patter of feet that scurried across her kitchen floors.

"David," she called again. "Didn't y'all hear me?"

I swear to the Lord Almighty that he is going deaf, she cussed in her head.

This wouldn't be surprising; as in a moment of trying to recapture his youth, David had brought an MP3 player off the internet. He blasted his player so loud these days that Geraldine was convinced her husband not only suffered from tinnitus but from deafness entirely.

"I'm gonna book him that damn ear test," she mumbled under her breath.

Geraldine turned to head downstairs to the basement, where David's sanctuary lay, but was stopped in her tracks by the sight of four little creatures.

"Sweet Mary mother of Jesus," she bellowed, sheer shock elevating her body.

The four little blue things in front of her were simply staring, wide eyed, like a puppy awaiting a treat from its master.

Geraldine had never been afraid of a little confrontation in her sometimes world-weary upbringing but the vision of these creatures was enough to make her reach for her broom and start thrashing it about wildly with blind fury.

Without her glasses on, though, she was severely disadvantaged, not that it mattered much as the little creatures ran for safety in every corner of the room.

Her screaming was enough to wake the dead but apparently not enough for David to hear. The little beings leapt up onto the kitchen side and launched themselves out of the window.

With that, they disappeared.

Without a trace.

Geraldine searched for her glasses, giving her a moment to catch her breath.

"David," she screamed. "You ain't gonna believe it. I think it was some rabid racoons from the fields...that or the Walton kids were playing havoc!"

She fixed her hair and grew instantaneously tried of David's basement hiding antics. So, without missing a beat, she made her way down to his hideout to give him a piece of what-for.

In all of the commotion, Geraldine missed something move behind her.

Something that was far more terrifying than four little blue beings.

*

Guadalajara, Mexico.

The boxer.

That was what he wanted to be known as.

Carlos 'The Boxer' Ramones.

As a child he had trained at every possible free second he had. His brother had shown him how to run properly, his father had given him his first pair of boxing gloves and his mother had dropped him off at every training session he had ever attended.

That was twenty years ago. Now, Carlos found himself chancing it in the ring for the biggest fight of his life. He had grown into one of the most talented boxers that his home town and prominent city had ever produced. He was in peak physical condition and nothing would stand in his way.

At this particular fight, only minutes away, the stakes couldn't have been higher. There was a huge wager placed on the match, riding high into the hundreds of thousands for some. Carlos himself stood to make a sizable portion… if he won.

Carlos stepped into the ring.

The bell rung.

Carlos, a southpaw, went straight in with an upper-cut.

His opponent counterpunched.

Carlos dodged, delivering a combination, finishing it with a hook.

They sparred, they parried.

It seemed an even match.

Until, the third round.

Carlos delivered a sucker-punch to the stomach, followed by three jabs, then a blow to the head, and finally he delivered the knock-out.

The referee counted his opponent out.

Carlos took the fight with a unanimous decision and with it; more financial success than he ever could have dreamed of.

His trainer, Juan, was the first to offer his congratulations. Then came his brother, his parents and finally his wife, Gabriella.

"I am so proud of you, Carlos," she practically screeched. "You have brought us so much; I don't deserve you, my angel, my hero."

Carlos panted heavily, the implications of the fight slowly catching up with his body. "Thank you, my sweetheart."

"What will we do with so much money? It is more than I have ever seen in my life."

"There is a lot we can do. First, a vacation?"

Gabriella laughed.

"There is one thing," Carlos said. "Now, seems like as good as time as any to do it. I have always wanted to start my own business."

Gabriella cocked her head. "Oh…of…of course. Of course."

"You will support me?"

"Yes, sweetheart."

"I don't deserve you."

"What business are you going to run? A restaurant? A boxing academy?"

"Comic books and video games."

The words fell on deaf ears.

"What?"

"I have written a comic book. Like the ones they make films into. I have done drawings for it also. And the video games, I'm reading how to create those, too."

"Have you lost your mind? Are you insane? Are you an idiot?"

"No…I thought…you said you would support me?"

"In something that will work! In something that isn't a boy's fantasy! What will your family say?"

"Who cares what my family says. This is what I want to do."

"But you're a boxer! You have such talent!"

"I think I am good at comic books also!"

"What about the baby?"

"What baby?"

"I'm pregnant."

Suddenly everything changed.

"You have a choice, Carlos, your silly little dream life or our baby."

Carlos assumed there wasn't a choice to make. He bent down and kissed Gabriella's belly.

Once for her.

Then a second time for the new life growing inside of her.

With a kiss for his love and new life, his hopes and ambitions of the future eroded into the past, decaying into an already faded black dream.

*

"I swear to God, David," she kept cursing as she trotted down the steps to his man lair.

She turned the corner and stopped. She felt herself go cold and stiff.

It couldn't be…

Seeping through the door of the basement was a thick stream of blood.

Geraldine felt the life drain out of her.

"David, David, David!"

She opened the door and dropped to her knees at the sight that lay before her.

Slumped on the floor in a lifeless heap was her beloved husband. She screamed with every ounce of fear in her body. She felt grief and devastation ripple through her bloodstream.

She scrambled back to her feet and ran to the side of her husband's corpse. She rolled David onto his side and felt herself fall back in horror.

For this wasn't David.

It was in the sense of his body but his charming face looked as if it had been ravaged by meat deprived wolves. His face was nothing more than soft, raw tissue, soaked in blood.

"No, dear God, no," Geraldine wailed, the tears cascading like a waterfall, refusing to end.

Creak. . Creak. . Creak.

Geraldine heard it.

Silence.

Then, breathing.

Heavy breathing.

The wolves were back, Geraldine thought. "Come out here, so I can slaughter y'all."

Nothing.

Geraldine could feel her heart working overtime.

Creak.

There was movement.

Geraldine looked up to the top of the staircase.

Concealed in the shadows was her husband's attacker. Geraldine could barely see who was there in the dim light of the staircase. She could just make out that something was standing, motionless, while it was watching her.

It was over seven-feet in height, parcelled with dripping blood from its fanged mouth. Its grotesque body seemed to pulsate with each breath.

Geraldine thought that her eyes were fooling her.

However, she knew that her ears were working perfectly when the creature let out a blood curdling scream that the even the Devil himself would be wary of.

The monstrous roar was a sound that Geraldine had never heard in her life before, and unfortunately for the much loved woman, it would also be her last.

CHAPTER FIVE

Four billion light-years away, idly drifting in the infinite extensions of silent space and shimmering stars lay a monstrously sized space ship. Its sleek design was nothing compared to the girth of the underbelly of the craft, its size was large enough to match a continent of Earth. Its torpedo-like engines at the rear of the ship would make even the most perspicacious of minds stand in utter perplexity. The ship in question was known in the native alien tongue as the *Bloodliner,* the now temporary refuge of the alien race known as The Xironets.

Inside the spacecraft, every hallway, every control room and medical bay was a hive of activity. This was a species in disarray. One could see their grotesque brains, which were visible from the back of the grasshopper-like heads, working overtime and contorting with confusion and panic.

This was a species on the run, fleeing their home world after its seismic implosion.

The Xironets could be impeccably described as a vision of sheer terror from a child's weeping nightmare. Their clawed feet could deliver killer blows in one swift stroke while their bulging torsos housed a hooved-shaped heart. Their seven foot statue was enough to work their appetites into hyper sensitivity while their fanged teeth sat in a mouth that a humanoid observer might describe as coming from a mythological dragon. Their moss-green bodies oozed with sweaty, stinking moisture that gave off a sulphuric stench to turn even the most hardened of stomachs.

The command deck at the epicentre of the ship bore technology that might not be seen on earth for another two-thousand years. The view screen that hung in the middle of the controls displayed that of a singular image; four little blue beings.

The Queen Xironet, a somewhat omnipresent figure in the alien's race, had been forced to reveal herself when the evacuation orders had come to her Temple.

The majority of Xironets believed The Queen was a mythical figure, and they also believed the truth to be that she had died centuries ago but was kept alive in stories to instil order and complacency into the species.

The Xironets only ever saw The King on occasions but now that had all changed. There were whispers that The King was slowly dying and that The Queen, who indeed existed, was now taking on the role of her partner. The Xironets had been ordered to cease training their young, halt all operations, withdraw from their tending of the wounded and launch a mass search for the four surviving members of their rival race.

The Xironets had begun to hear rumblings that the Leader of the rival clan was dead, that he had perished on their home world of Zolandor. If this was true, then it was at the utmost severity to find the missing blue beings.

Some believed in the strange magic that was supposed to take place between the two species. One of the folklores that had been passed down was that The King Xironet and leader of the blue beings could consciously communicate through some sort of spiritual transcendence. If this was true, then why couldn't The King simply use these powers to find the AWOL stowaways? One rumour that was circulating on the ship was that perhaps because The King was dying, his skills were also failing with him.

The Queen had ordered search pods to be dispatched to any colonized world that was neighbouring their former home world. The *Bloodliner's* scanners hadn't detected any life readings from space which could only mean that they had taken refuge on an alien planet. It took a while for the viewport to light up but when it did, the alien beasts found themselves in disbelief. One of their colleagues was relaying a message back from his search pod.

He'd located a trace of the blue beings. He'd pick up the hint of a scent.

The Commander on deck reported this message to Her Highness The Queen. In turn, she told the Commander that they were to set course to the planet that the blue creatures had been found on and that they should prepare for immediate landing. The Commander was then informed to control the whispering of her subordinates as it could create insurmountable fear in a time when they needed to be strong.

What The Queen told the Commander next, however, was something that he wasn't prepared for; finding the beings was only their first goal and it was what the little blue beings had in their possession that was secretly the ultimate goal.

Whatever the little beings had…it was obviously of the utmost importance.

*

The sight of a spaceship in a park would have disturbed most people. The geeks weren't most people however and the fact that they had entered the spaceship and found no alien life completely scared the living daylights out of them.

The young geeks ran as fast as their under-exercised legs could carry them. They jumped over the brow of the river and tucked themselves down low beneath the grass. For some strange reason, each of the boys shared the same impulse that their ordeal was far from yet over.

"What do we do?" Chilvers quipped, barely audible over his gasping for oxygen.

"Why don't we just cover it up?" Mark suggested, his mind racing with fear. He couldn't help but feel a surging through his blood, a surge that felt like he was going to die. He shook the thought quickly from his mind.

Tom's eyes darted all over the place like he was trying to chase the bullets in a Wild West shoot out. "I say we call the press," he exclaimed.

"And tell them what?" Chilvers protested. "That we just happened to find an alien spaceship in the woods with no aliens. They'll laugh in our face. Get real."

"I agree," piped Matt. "This whole thing is ridiculous."

"They won't! This'll make us famous. Did you see the inside of that thing? No way that this thing is a hoax!"

"Pull it together, Tom," Chilvers said. "I agree with you that it does look...very....hm...convincing. But do you see any aliens? I don't see any aliens."

"Does anyone want my opinion?" Mark asked.

"Not really," hissed Tom.

Mark's opinion had never been taken for as long as he could remember but he didn't really mind.

If the geeks were a boy band, then Chilvers was the frontman, leading them with all his gusto and untapped greatness. Matt was the lead guitarist, the right hand man, the one who the group couldn't function without. Tom took on the role of the drummer, the one who was always apparently on the edge of life and the fans would always be talking about him with his latest scandal. That left Mark in the role of the bloke with no name. He was the band member who was always cropped out of pictures and left in the darkness on stage. The screaming girls would never chase him or hunt him down for his autograph. He was the one who would ultimately leave the band and no one would care. He'd retire from the industry and fade into the abyss of nothingness. The latter idea was sounding considerably promising to Mark right now.

So, here they were, on the cusp of a discovery like no other. Whatever this heap of metal turned out to be, it was most definitely going to be one that would go down in their history books.

Mark would let the other three bicker about the plan and when they reached a conclusion, he would follow their decision. He took that role well. Some called it 'easy-going' but Mark preferred the term; 'not bothered either way'.

In these normal situations, Mark would check the latest movie news on his phone or look at girls he liked on social media but since he lost in the wilderness of a spaceship, he was left to wonder to himself and look at nature. *How turgid*, he noted to himself. *Outside is vastly overrated.*

Mark strolled over to a few trees, carefully not wanting to stray too far from the group. There was, after all, a massive UFO sitting a few yards away from them. He occasionally picked up on what some of what his friends were saying and smiled when he realised that the fame-hungry Tom was still pleading to call the media. Mark was taking a particular interest in Matt's plan of just going home and forgetting the whole thing. But he didn't mind what they did and continued to amble on down to the river. He knelt down and dipped his hands in the cool water, splashing some on his worn face.

This was the closest thing that Mark would get to having a shower today as he didn't like bathing himself too often. Most teenage boys didn't follow the necessary hygiene rules of everyday life but Mark felt that he didn't really have any need to wash himself. He didn't really sweat because he never went faster enough to work one up. Plus, he had heard that women liked the rugged type of man, so he felt that being some-what dirty was all part of the appeal.

He suddenly jerked his head up from the river. He turned over to the left and squinted in the distance. He couldn't see very well since his glasses had been badly damaged with all the day's bruising.

Something moved.

Mark spun around, not quite being able to place where the noise was coming from, while, somehow, it seemed to be coming from all around.

Then, something caught his eye.

The bushes rustled.

A fox...? He thought. He hoped.

He took his glasses off to squint in vein of trying to make out what was causing the sound. Mark had never had 20/20 vision and feared that by the time he was forty he would be completely blind. *Curse my stunted eye sight,* he thought. This was also why he refrained from masturbating...to prevent the blindness that his grandmother warned him about every Sunday after church.

The noises grew louder. The blurs he could make out grew closer until finally they placed themselves in front of him. He felt the oxygen stop entering his lungs as his entire body entered a state of fear-induced trembling.

Mark stared hard. Without knowing that he was doing it, his hands slowly raised themselves to his eyes and gave them a rub. He reopened them only to be greeted with the same sight; that of four little blue beings.

The creatures didn't move but instead they looked up at Mark with a slight tilt in their tiny heads. He tried to speak but the words failed to register and nothing came out. With cautious movements, he slowly started to back away.

With his dire eyesight fixated on the alien beings before him, Mark missed the rock behind him and fell to the ground with a heavy thud, catching his back legs on the rock and shredding them as he fell.

Unhelpfully, another fragment of rock was placed just behind him in order to break the fall of his head and he cried out in agony as he felt the impact of his skull on exposed rock. He couldn't even register the pain, though, as through squinted eyes, he saw that the creatures were coming towards him.

Chilvers, Matt and Tom turned to see where their chubby little cohort was. It was then that their mouths fell agape in unison.

There was no denying now that the heap of charred metal to the side of them was that of alien existence. They instinctively dashed over to Mark to help him to his feet.

They knew that it was going to be this moment that would go on to be the defining seconds of their young lives.

There was no going back now.

Stood before the four geeks were four little blue beings. Neither race moved or said a word. A photographer would have given his life to have the picture, but thankfully, it was only the boys and aliens present. In what became an inconceivably astonishing game of live chess, the boys waited to see who would make the first move; them or the aliens.

*

Bristol, England.

Caroline stood at the back of the decrepit pub, nervously clutching a pint of questionably acidic cider in one hand and a withered piece of paper in the other.

She did a quick head count, not counting herself or the landlord, and she estimated that there were nine punters sat in the pub, all of whom were facing the dreaded, infamous purple curtain.

The current performer standing under the failing spotlight pranced across the stage, trying desperately to not drop the seemingly ancient microphone, held together by duct tape and elastic bands. Caroline had approximately three minutes until her name was called to go up on-stage and right now, every bone in her body was screaming at her to run out of the ghastly pub and hide under the duvet.

She had booked the day off work to go to a dying pub in the middle of a trade-losing street in an attempt to fulfil what her soul so desperately craved. *WHAT THE HELL WAS SHE THINKING?*

There was no turning back now, though. Caroline had spent six months writing and perfecting her debut stand-up comedy routine, and it was almost time to share what she thought would make people laugh with these half-baked alcoholics.

Caroline was thirty-two and ever since she could remember, she loved two things; comedy and Japanese Anime.

She had geeked out at every chance she had gotten when the frenzy of this particular pop-culture phenomenon had taken over. She was now at a level of love for Anime that she liked to call; an unprecedented level of fanaticism.

Caroline had taken herself off to all of the nationwide Comic-Con's dressed as her favourite characters and had even met her fiancé whilst attending an independent Japanese convention. This alone had stunned her, as Caroline had always been a loner. She drifted from job to job after college and had never really held any life-long friends, and so, she had no one to share her passions with.

This brought her to her love of comedy. Her father had shown her old episodes of an American sitcom called *Mork and Mindy* starring Robin Williams. She loved the euphoria of careless laughter and escapism, she too, hoping one day to bring a smile to people's faces.

She then trawled the archives to discover what would become her lifelong favourite comedies; the long-running American sketch show *Saturday Night Live,* the 1990's U.S sitcom, *Home Improvement,* starring Tim Allen.

As she grew older, Caroline had discovered British classics such as *Bottom, Blackadder* and *Mr. Bean.*

Eventually, Caroline started to appreciate the show *Whose Line Is It Anyway?,* and it was through watching the cult favourite that she really wanted to tread the boards of the working class pubs and clubs and make audiences laugh.

But what to talk about? She had debated covering the general topics of relationships, sex and politics but deep down she knew she could write a breadth of material about the most tantalizing of all subjects; Anime.

So, here she stood, moments away from arriving on stage to stand in front of midday drunkards who would not have a clue what she was talking about. But if she could just make a connection, to touch one person and raise a smile, then, just then, she might feel a tinge of contentment inside.

And with that, the MC called her name, and Caroline made her way from the darkness and into the blinding lights of the stage.

The lights of a better future.

*

Minutes passed with no respite from the tension. The boys looked down at the blue bundles of mass and the aliens looked up at the gawky looking boys towering above them.

Finally, Chilvers couldn't wait any longer. "Do we run?"

None of them could take their eyes away from the creatures before them. They were no more than two-foot in height, with rounding bellies on each of them. Their tiny humanoid heads were accentuated by protruding foreheads like nothing any of the boys had ever seen before. Their skin, or what the boys presumed was skin, seemed to glow a beautiful shade of sky-blue. Meanwhile, their white, beady eyes were like that of an infant. It all made for a rather bemusing, yet captivating appearance.

As Chilvers' words slowly registered with the other boys, they slowly willed their lips to move and acquire any semblance of sound but it became apparent that there was no time for anyone to reply. The taller of the two-foot high creatures let out a war like scream with its tongue, delivering a rapid-fire delivery of noises.

"Too late," Matt gulped.

And then, with fluid and unfathomable motion, it began to happen.

One of the aliens stepped forward and the boys couldn't help but notice how elegant and relaxed the little being moved. It was almost as if it was gracefully gliding through a cloud, in a dream-like tranquil state. The blue being then raised its index finger and began to mutter something in its own language. The boys watched on in unsurmountable trepidation as the finger then began to scan each of the boys.

Good God, Chilvers thought. *It's picking its prey.*

Tom's mind went into overdrive, searching for the rights words. "What would Harrison Ford do?"

The finger pointed at each of the boys in turn, wavering between them. But it didn't stay fixated on any one of the boys in particular for too long. The alien finger scanned again, and then the being closed his eyes until it finally began to leisurely rock its digit back and forth like a ball bearing beginning to grind to a halt.

Then, stillness.

The finger didn't move. It seemed contented with whom it had picked.

Mark.

"Tell my parents," Mark began. "That I knew I was a failure." His eyes glistened with wetness as his voice broke to a delicate whisper.

The other boys could only watch helplessly as the tiny finger then began to radiate superlative neon blue. The being then seemed to start chanting. Then, one by one, the other three beings began to join in.

Of all the ways he thought he would die, Mark's demise by a two inch alien finger was not of them. He had considered the fact that he might choke to death on one of his beloved chocolate fingers but not an alien one.

The space around the little creatures then began to swirl with electric blue energy as a cacophony of colours started to billow around them as if doing some tribal dance in the days of old.

"What is this?" Chilvers whispered to himself.

Matt could only watch. There were no words he could think of. And if there were, they didn't seem fitting.

Tom's eyes were filled with a mixture of two things: concern for his friend and a strange sensation of joy. "I think this is some kind of other-worldly power."

And then, a powerful surge of vehemence alien force shot itself from the alien hand and made its way towards

Mark. It encompassed him like the arms of a loved one whom had not seen their companion in a lifetime.

The intensified weight of the energy became incontestable, thus it threw the other three boys to the floor as it continued to engulf Mark.

He then began to be lifted off the floor, seemingly unaided except for anything other than the alien energy. There were tears in his eyes that desperately wanted to escape but he managed to hold them back a little longer.

The other boys watched as Mark's floating body made its way towards the finger of the little alien.

"I think he's wet himself," Tom murmured, noticing the wet patch on Mark's crotch.

"I think I've shit myself," Matt replied.

The hovering Mark was then brought to a grinding halt a foot away from the rhapsodic alien finger. The following three seconds of nothingness seemed to last forever, until finally, a surge of blinding white light erupted from the alien and shot directly to Mark.

The verve of a million lifetimes swapped around him like a hurricane stampeding through a city. After thirty seconds, the illumination reached its crescendo and shot back out of Mark to retreat towards the emblematic being who possessed the power. Finally, Mark was safely lowered to the floor.

Chilvers couldn't catch his breath. He quickly eyed his chubby friend and felt a wave of relief rush over him when he saw Mark's stomach was moving, albeit slowly.

He was alive. But, what had all this just been? Chilvers remarked to himself. He timidly took a few steps toward Mark, at the same time keeping a close eye on the four little creatures.

Chilvers bent down to Mark's side. *Could it be? How is that possible?* All the bruises, cuts and scars that Mark had gained throughout the day had been healed. Not a single cut on him. Even his glasses had been perfectly restored. *Had the little aliens cured him? Helped him? Healed him?*

Chilvers looked up to see that Matt and Tom were motioning towards the aliens. Chilvers turned and saw that they were taking tiny steps towards them, seemingly not wanting to scare the boys away. The aliens began muttering and chirping away but the boys simply stared back, an overwhelming sense that a history making moment having being played out before them.

"What do you think they're saying?" Tom quipped.

"I have no idea," replied Matt.

Mark got to his feet and checked himself all over. He looked at his glasses, now born again. The aliens had slightly corrected his fraying vision. "Maybe, they said that…"

"What we communicated," spoke a deep, sombre, yet wise voice. "We communicated to each of our fellow beings here that we have helped your friend. And in return for our gesture of kindness, we plead that you return this act."

Matt felt a rush of blood bombard his head. "I don't believe it. You…you…speak our language?"

"We do," the alien voice replied. "Now, do you consider our request?"

Well fuck me, Chilvers thought. Was a tiny little alien being asking his friends and himself for help? Chilvers felt his throat tighten.

"Please, we do not have any time to waste. We beg you for your help. You have our word that you will be given a full explanation."

Chilvers eyed the other boys. Everyone looked as if they had all just done some hard core LSD and hadn't slept in a month.

What would Ford do now?

And then, as close friends tend to do, they all seemed to read each other's minds. They knew what each other was thinking. With one single nod, they had reached their conclusion.

"You sure?" Chilvers said, allowing a wicked grin to spread across his face.

The boys nodded.

Their fates were sealed.

And with that, geeks and aliens ran off into the woods.

Some may question their decision to help extraterrestrial life but in hindsight, there was never any question about it. These were aliens. And they were geeks. There was only ever going to be one answer.

Mark made sure he lagged at the back with a slow pace.

Better they don't pick up on the smell of shit from my pants. Damn it, he cursed to himself. *How un-Ford like...*

CHAPTER SIX

1.58.pm.

Surprisingly for England, the sun had made an appearance and seemed determined to stick around for a little while longer.

Office workers on their lunch breaks stole a few minutes away from their desks to enjoy a walk outside and a few even found themselves in a secluded beer garden, far, far away from the watchful eye of an all-seeing boss.

At the far end of the busy road lay a derelict construction site. The council had fronted a lot cash for a new, lush, series of apartments but they had eventually run out of money.

No money; no builders.

This expansive wasteland was now home to those who found themselves without a place to call home and the occasional drug deal could be found taking place at the west side on the entrance.

It was also now home to four gawky looking teenagers and their...stowaways.

The now doubled foursome had managed to make their way through the woods and backstreets, ducking and diving out of view of any prying eyes. That had been the easy part; getting to the town centre.

The problem now lay in the fact that all four of the boys lived on the other side of the main hub of the town and they had no clue how to get to their desired destination without being seen.

For now, their alien counterparts were tucked away, hidden behind sacks of cement mix and broken bricks. They had not vocally communicated with the apparent leader of the race since they had made a dash for it, partly leading the boys to consider the fact that perhaps they had had their morning juice spiked at school this morning.

But as time wore on...apparently all of what they saw before them was real.

Good Lord.

Matt checked his watch whilst still peering at the new arrivals from the corner of his eye. "So, what's the plan? We can't just keep them here."

"We might be able to lay low here for a while," Tom suggested, eyes beaming with pure happiness. He then adjusted his voice to that of a stage whisper. "CAN YOU ACTUALLY BELIEVE WHAT IS HAPPENING?"

"I know," Mark replied. "My family should have moved to these apartments years ago if the council hadn't have run out of money."

"I MEANT THE FUCKING ALIENS YOU PRICK! NOT THE FUCKING ESTATE!"

"Calm down," Chilvers snapped. "Everybody, just take a breath and calm down. Our friends seem okay for the time being. And, I don't know how you guys feel, but I really don't feel threatened by them. I don't think they're dangerous at all...it's..."

"It's almost like there's a connection, right?" Matt agreed.

Tom rubbed his beardless chin. "I was thinking on the run over...it's almost as if...they chose us?"

Mark shook his head. "To think, I could have bloody lived here...it would have been perfect for spying on your Aunty, Chilvers!"

"Enough with this bloody place, Mark," Tom snarled. "We don't care that you almost lived here. We are on the brink of making history and you..."

"You're a genius, Mark!" Chilvers declared.

"He's a fucking what?"

"He's a genius. My Aunty. She's only a few streets away. She works full time. I can shoot over to hers, double check she's out and we can hide our new friends there for a while."

Matt suddenly perked up. "Sounds good to me. Anything is better than here. I know it's out of the way but it still feels kind of exposed. If anyone comes by, we're done for."

"Good call," Tom concurred. "We'll hold the fort here and see if we can pry any information from these creatures. Although I don't feel in danger, I'd still like to know...well...more."

"For the love of God, don't do anything stupid," Chilvers announced. And with that, he picked himself up and ran as fast as his gangly legs would carry him.

*

Atlantic City, New Jersey.

The door clicked.

The house grew still.

The occupants living here on Woodridge Avenue each closed their eyes and prayed that they would perhaps be spared any punishment that was coming.

Ashleigh and her younger brother, Dylan, knew the drill inside out.

Their father would come home from his nightly gambling session, every time on a losing streak, and then search the cupboards in search of alcohol. If he cracked a beer open, they might be spared, as he quite often fell asleep almost instantaneously. If he reached for a bottle, usually vodka or scotch, then they knew to both ready themselves for the sound of the deafening screams of their Mother as she desperately tried to defend herself.

Sister and brother held each other as they waited for the sound…a *popping* sound…followed by *glugging.*

Bottle it was. It was at this time that the duo separated.

Ashleigh went to her room to listen to her IPod. It was here that she was able to drown out the wailing pain of her Mother.

Dylan, aged eight, would retreat to his room, lock the door, and pick up his Grandfather's old video camera. The camera was once used to record happy family occasions, birthdays and Christmases, times that people would want to remember, now however, the only recordings being made on the old machine were those that Dylan chose to create.

Every night, he would draw out which story he wanted to tell. He would then allow the bliss of his fantasies to flood him, taking him far away from the Devil that was downstairs in the kitchen.

Dylan would animate little characters of toys and drawings, stopping and starting the camera, fractionally moving each of the pieces each frame to create a stop-motion effect, thus, when the images were played in their entirety, it seemed like they were moving.

It was here, mind focused on making little cartoons and entering a finite utopia, that Dylan briefly found childhood happiness, almost as if a small piece of Heaven had been handed down to him, allowing the frightened little boy to run away, far away, from the crushing reality that awaited him in the hours to come.

For a few moments, the budding filmmaker felt as if everything was going to be okay.

*

An out-of-breath Chilvers arrived a few doors away from his Aunt's house. It was a spacious home, well, more of a show home that was situated directly opposite the town's best loved Chinese takeaway.

His unmarried Aunty was a born and bred working class lass who loved nothing more than a good piss-up and party. In order to fund this alcohol loving lifestyle, she worked every hour God sent at the supermarket.

Whenever his Aunty visited his home, Chilvers always unsuccessfully drowned out the news about her latest boyfriend or toy boy, instead choosing to notice how haggard his Aunty was now looking, the heavy drinking clearly taking its toll on her appearance.

Chilvers arrived at the front door. He had always had a key to her home on his chain, his mother was worried that one day her sister would need assistance after falling down the stairs drunk, so she trusted Chilvers with a key.

The plan was to open the door, have a quick look around, double check the attic was still used to store the Christmas decorations and then go get his friends to hide the blue beings away while they brought some time.

Chilvers took a tentative step forward and gently slipped the key into the lock. He opened the door and tiptoed his way into his Aunt's home.

What he found though, was the single most traumatic scene he had ever witnessed in his short lived life.

*

At the construction site, Matt, Mark and Tom quietly sat observing the blue creatures. Tom had edged close to the beings but couldn't bring himself to disturb them as they appeared to have fallen into some kind of meditative trance.

"What do you think they're doing?"

"I don't know…some kind of…ritual?"

"Should we speak to them?"

"We could…we don't know anything about them. We know they need help and we know…well…I think we can safely state that we know they are…um…aliens? We've agreed to help them…I think we deserve to know some answers."

"Okay, fine, if we…"

Their inquisition was interrupted, however, when Chilvers barged through the gangway. His hair was wild from the run and his eyes spoke the story of a man who had seen too much.

Matt raised his eyebrows. "What happened to you?"

"Yeah, you look like shit," Mark added.

"I…she…Aunty…me…there…I…all…"

"What the hell are you on about?"

"My Aunty, she was home."

"Oh, okay."

"And she's a swinger."

"What?"

"I've said too much. I've seen too much. We have to go, we have to leave now."

"Calm down, calm down. Wait a second, what do you mean she…"

"WE NEVER MENTION THIS AGAIN. NOW, LET'S GO!"

"We've got nowhere to go, we can't go now anyway!"

"Why not?"

"They're doing some…alien things…look!"

Chilvers turned his gaze towards the aliens. They sat on the floor in a huddle, gently swaying to an apparent beat that the geeks couldn't hear. In their clipped alien tongue, they seemed to be talking not to one another, but in unison. As if chanting.

"I just don't know what to do; the only place I know that will be free of people is my house. My parents don't get home from work until early evening and my sister is away at university. It's the best place I can think of but I don't know how to get there without being seen or stopped…or worse."

Matt looked solemnly to the floor then barked his head up. "I have an idea. I know how we can get them to yours in the cover of daylight. It's perfect."

"How?"

"My ex-girlfriend," Matt replied.

A cumulative gasp erupted.

"Your what?"

"You never told us about this?"

"You dog, you."

"It was months ago," Matt stated. "It was with Jessica Loot."

This aroused further, greater gasps.

"WITH WHO?"

The other boys' shock was to be understood. Jessica Loot was the most stunning girl, not only in their school year, but in the entire student body. Every testosterone driven teenage boy ogled over her and spent sleepless nights wishing that she was theirs to belong to. She was, for all intents and purposes, perfect in every way. Quite what she was doing going on a date with Matt simply befuddled the mind in new ways.

Chilvers coughed a cough to move the conversation forward. "Well, go on!"

"I have to admit that I was only her boyfriend for a few hours and to be honest…it was only pretend.

"You see, she wanted to go with Daniel Troves but for obvious reasons, her parents wouldn't allow it. They didn't approve of his…um…lewd behaviour. So, one day she said she was looking for a foil. She was looking for the most uninteresting, un-charming, unattractive and repulsive boy she could think of. And that boy was me.

"So, she took me back to meet her parents and introduced me as her boyfriend. They seemed to love me and I very quickly loved her. They gave us their blessing and said we could go out to movies. Obviously, there were no movies, so we walked outside where she dumped me and Daniel Troves picked her up. I had to walk home in the pouring rain where I subsequently got mugged."

"That's cold."

"That's hurtful."

"That bitch," Mark stated.

"I don't mind, replied Matt. "She said I could ask one favour in return. There are certain things I can't ask for but pretty much she said that anything goes."

"I don't see how this will help us?"

"She and her family are hikers. Outdoorsy kind of people. They have walking gear. And more importantly, they have backpacks. Four of them. Perfect to put our friends in and get to Tom's." Matt proclaimed all of this with a genuine, heartfelt smile that beamed with pride. "Now, I'm off."

*

Through the hidden blankets of space and time, the Xironets gargantuan spacecraft blasted its way towards its desired destination.

The crew aboard the ship had been informed of very little. The beasts were fully aware that one of their own had only missed the little blue beings by a short amount of time but unfortunately, the hunter had lost the trail again.

The enwreathed Queen had subsequently ordered that the incompetent fool who had failed to capture their diminutive enemies was to be held accountable for his misgivings and was to be executed on sight. Though the Xironets were aggressive beasts by nature, this was a new era of sadistic barbarity even for them.

The crew and last surviving members of their race, which ran to nearly seven-hundred-and-eighty-thousand, had then received an official order. This was no longer a simple forage mission, it was reconnaissance.

They were looking for something. And not just the little aliens.

Something that the blue creatures had on their possession.

Once said entity was retrieved, it was then to become far more than an earth invasion…it was to become a mass extermination.

*

Denver, Colorado.

The past twenty-years had slipped through their hands with no forgiveness. If there had been an hour-glass, then, it surely would have broken at the speed in which the years had ticked by.

For Jake and Ben, however, they were still the best friends that they had been when they had met aged five. Now, they were a quarter of a century old, and both were facing the prospect of turning the page to a new chapter in their lives.

Their respective girlfriends were out on a birthday bar crawl with one of their colleagues from work, but to be honest, the pair didn't really pay attention. All that mattered was the fact that it was to be a man's night in with a movie, beer and pizza.

Perfect.

Jake and Ben had grown up together and shared the highs and lows that any family members would; they had shared in each other's joys, harboured each other's pain and watched the others backs until the sun had come up and the day was done.

Like most children, they had become friends over very little, the ability to play and run around was enough to seal a friendship for life but as they had grown older, the pair had become something known as cos-players. They had spent hundreds, even thousands of dollars, on replica costumes of their favourite characters from their most beloved films and T.V shows. They had even won some awards.

Four years ago, whilst attending San Diego Comic-Con, they had both plucked up the courage to speak to two girls; those girls would eventually move in with them and set up a life together.

Though work and life had occasionally pulled them apart, Jake and Ben were as tight as they had been all those years ago.

In truth, one didn't know where they'd be without the other.

Jake cracked the beers while Ben set up a movie and readied the takeout pizza. They eased into the recliners and slurped on their beverages.

"Cheers."

"Cheers."

They watched the movie for a while, taking themselves back ten years ago when they had first seen it.

"Wonder how the women are getting on?" Jake mused.

"I've put a sick bowl and kitchen towel out for Harriet, just in case," Ben replied.

"Good call, Kathy can't really handle her booze like she used too," Jake scoffed.

Ben started laughing to himself. "Remember that time that we all went bowling and Harriet was so drunk she puked up in the bowling ball then hurled it down the lane. Sick was everywhere."

"Oh, God. I tried to block that out. I gotta admit it was a little embarrassing. What had she had to drink?"

"One tequila," Ben blurted out with laughter, a little pizza flying over the chair.

Jake finished off his can and pulled out two more from the fridge. "So, you guys all set for your trip to Europe? I wish we could come but work is so burning right now, my boss would go psycho if I went travelling."

Ben suddenly looked struck with an invisible pain. He put his beer down and paused the movie. "Funny thing about that," he said. "I've been meaning to talk to you about that trip."

"What, you not going now?"

"Oh, yeah, sure, we're going."

"So?"

"It's just that…we're going for a little longer than planned."

"Sweet. How long?"

"Um…like…permanent."

Jake raised an eyebrow, waiting for the punchline.

It didn't come.

Jake's expression dropped. "Wait, you're serious?"

"Yeah, Harriet got a job offer in Germany. It's too good to turn down. We talked a lot about it and I obviously need to go with her."

"So, you're just leaving? When do you go?"

"That's the funny thing; you see part of the deal for getting this job was that she starts straight away. So, we're…um…leaving on Friday."

"What the fuck? Why are you just telling this me now?"

"I didn't wanna talk about it, pal. I knew how difficult it would be. I don't wanna say goodbye to you."

"Well, then, don't go."

"It's not that simple. I'm gonna propose to Harriet and hopefully start a family. We both knew that we couldn't stay kids forever. I'm sorry, buddy."

"I don't want you to go. You're my best friend."

"We'll always be best friends. It'll just be a little different, I guess. This is something I gotta do, pal. I hope you understand. I'll carry our friendship with me everywhere. Don't start thinking this is something about us falling out or something."

"I'm just a little stunned that's all. It's a lot to take in. I'm gonna miss you, buddy."

"I'm gonna miss you too. I've never had a friend like you. You're my blood brother."

"I can't believe it. It's going to be so weird. Not having you here. I won't like it. I don't wanna say goodbye."

"You don't think I'm not scared of leaving? I'm absolutely terrified."

Jake rubbed his head. "Wait, if you leave on Friday, then...this is our last time hanging out together."

"Yeah."

"So...what do we do?"

"Enjoy it I guess. It's not a goodbye, just a farewell for a long time. Well, that's one way of looking at it. Glass half full, right?"

"What do you wanna do?"

Ben paused, his mind turning. "I got an idea."

Half an hour later, they were both sat on the recliners still watching a movie, eating pizza and drinking beer, only they were dressed a little different.

Ben had dug out their last Comic-con costumes; two *Stormtroopers* from *Star Wars.* So, there they sat, enjoying each other's company for what could possibly be the last time.

After the film finished, they sat in silence for a while, both men searching for the right words but not quite finding them.

Then, Ben simply said what was on his mind. "You know I love you, pal? Right? I love you more than most of my own fucking family."

Jake laughed, being careful not to spill any beer down his thousand–dollar costume. "Don't get soppy on me, bitch. By the way, if you ever come back to Denver and look me up and I find out that you've gone to Comic-Con with someone else, then I will kill you."

"Deal."

"Deal."

And there they sat, twenty-years of laughter and friendship about to draw to a close, but they both knew, deep down, that they wouldn't have a changed a minute of it for anything in the world.

*

2.36.pm.

The words that came out of Matt's mouth when he returned were simple and to the point; "I fucking hate running."

None of them could deny this statement. They had all done far more cardio workout in the space of three hours than they had in their entire lives. All of the boys had passionately protested against their father's wishes for them to start playing football.

Aside from the horrific notion of physical endurance, all the boys found the idea of the *beautiful game* a little too…homoerotic. Lots of young men running around getting sweaty…*no thank you.* The most exertive and strenuous physical activity the boys did was trying to relieve a severe bout of constipation. The geeks were far more interested in trying to win over girls with the expansive knowledge of comic books and movie minutia.

The geeks also spent countless hours in the library, vicariously studying the female form and the inner cognitive workings of the opposite sexes mind.

Of course, it unequivocally went over their young heads to actually go out and talk to a girl but they wouldn't be where they were now if they were members of the elite social clicks.

Matt produced four back packs.

Chilvers couldn't help but embrace his friend. "This is perfect. You've come up trumps here, my pal."

He then produced four pairs of running shoes.

"Oh, for fucks sake," Mark chimed. "More running! What for?"

"To give the appearance that we are jogging on our way somewhere with bags full of stuff! People will think we're…in training for something!"

Tom took a pair of the trainers. "He's right. For all we know the spaceship back in the woods might have already been discovered and people might be asking questions. As little suspicion as possible, that's our goal."

"Right then, what's the plan?" Matt asked.

"Once we make it to your safe hideout," came a calm, distant voice. "We will elaborate on our presence here, along with events that have transpired and happenings we believe are forthcoming."

The geeks stared at the blue beings that were now stood side by side, eyes transfixed on each of the boys.

Chilvers opened his mouth, hoping for sound. "We…you…um…"

"I think what he's trying to say is…" Tom interrupted. "Is that…this is still a little strange for us. We're here…with four aliens…"

"Please…we are the Wongtoks."

"Oh…um…I see…pleasure to meet you."

Bewilderment settled for a few moments, the Wongtoks seemingly understanding that the situation must have felt like a snapshot in a dream, caught somewhere between sleep and awake.

Chilvers jilted his head. "Right, we could do this all day. We need to move and we need to move now."

His friends nodded and opened their backpacks to allow the Wongtoks to climb in. They suited up, tied their trainers and headed out into the open.

They settled into a light jogging pace that was just quick enough for them to make it look like they did this exercising malarkey every day, whilst being virulent not to pull any fragile ligaments.

After a while, Tom couldn't help but feel a pull towards a sense of laughter. "You know something," he said, panting as he ran. "These…Wongtoks…they would make awesome toys."

The others laughed at the absurdity, carefully masking their own secret thoughts that they too, had allowed the idea to drop into their heads.

CHAPTER SEVEN

The boys arrived within touching distance of Tom's home and with their hope slowly reaching new heights, there lay only a small glitch in the plan. He lived in a quiet street that was mainly inhabited by retired residents, thus they were always home.

Thus, they saw everything.

Thus, they knew everyone's business.

There was no way they could get to his front door without arousing a whiff of suspicion. For the time being, the boys and bundled-up backpacks took to crouching behind an alleyway, looking like the motley crew that they had been so destined to become.

Tom glanced at his watch. "If we go now, the neighbours will tell my parents that I was home before school was out."

Matt raised a lopsided smile. "We're harbouring alien fugitives in backpacks. I think your neighbour's gossiping is the least of our worries."

"I suppose. Point taken."

Chilvers concurred. "I say we just do it. Tom, you go check no one's home and we'll-"

Chilvers heard something. The others heard it too.

Voices coming from down the alleyway, only slightly behind them.

"We're going to have to go now," Tom reluctantly agreed, hearing the approaching voices coming closer. He edged forward to the end of the alleyway, spying his house. No cars. His folks were still at work. Perfect. It almost would be, except for the sight of Deidre making her way directly towards them. "Oh, shit."

"What?"

"We've got company from both sides." He eyed the broken fence panel. "Quick, hide behind there and wait for them to pass. Then, we go to my house."

The four boys quickly squeezed through the fence, it feeling like a tighter spot than it originally looked.

They waited for Deidre to pass, which she did, ambling along at quite a remarkable speed for an elderly lady.

Then they just had to wait for...*Rigger*? There was no mistaking the voice of their tormentor from school.

Mark rolled his eyes at the sound of his bully's banal tone.

"*This is a quiet spot, yeah, blood,*" they heard him say.

"I think he's with someone," Tom whispered.

"Well, whoever he's with, let's hope they go quick, my knees are killing me and I don't think I can stay crouched for too long," Chilvers said, grimacing through the pain.

"He's probably doing a drug deal or something."

They remained as quiet as they could, the last thing they needed was for Rigger, of all people, to find them.

"*Look, I don't know how long I can be doing this,*" Rigger began, sounding more distressed with every syllable.

"*I know, I know, it's killing me too,*" came the male reply. The boys couldn't make out who it was through the hushed tones.

"*I don't like this being a secret no more though, bruv.*"

Bruv? The geeks knew there was only one person that Rigger referred to as bruv and that person was Burnsey. Whatever their secret was, the geeks silently smiled that they were about to be let in on it.

"*What more can I say, bruv, I love you. I want people to know that we is a couple.*"

Oh.

The geeks weren't expecting that.

Not in the slightest.

Rigger and Burnsey were a couple?

This was a juicy bit of gossip like no other.

The geeks peaked their ears to the fence, gaining a better advantage to listen in.

"Think of our street cred! No way is I going to tell people."

"So you is ashamed of our love then, yeah?"

"No, I is just...bruv...I just..."

"Don't bruv me! I has a heart too, yeah!"

From the behind the fence, the creases in Mark's forehead were working overtime, a sign he was confused. "Do you think that they're gay?" he questioned, always the last to figure out the obvious.

Chilvers couldn't hide his sarcasm. "Yes, I think that's what we've picked up. Rigger and Burnsey are-"

"We is what?"

The boys looked up, their vision blocked by the sight of Rigger towering over them. "Get out here now you little pussy holes."

The geeks did as commanded, filing out one by one. Rigger and Burnsey stood before them, looking flustered with a tinge of anger.

"I is gonna say this once," Rigger stated. "If you say a word of this to anyone then you is all dead."

The geeks held their ground. After all, they had nothing to lose.

They finally had an ace card to play and it was time to use it. Tom took the lead. "On the contrary, my closeted friend, if either of you dare ever try to lay a hand on us ever again, or if you ever try to torment us ever again... then we will tell the whole school your secret. And I mean...the whole school."

"You pricks wouldn't dare."

"Try us," Tom replied with a cock-sure wink.

Rigger and Burnsey simply stared, the hatred for the geeks clearly rising but deep down fully aware that the boys were no longer afraid.

"Get out of here you fucking shits."

"As a new dawn of freedom begins for us, we, the geeks, will no longer-"

"Don't overdo it, Tom," Chilvers remarked. "Bring it down."

"Yeah, I suggest you listen to your bum chum."

"Rigger," Chilvers smirked. "Fuck you!"

Satisfied that they had finally won a small victory over the big man, the geeks turned and headed to Tom's house.

*

The boys entered through Tom's front door. They wasted no time in taking off their rucksacks and opening them up to reveal their alien stowaways.

Matt checked them over, much like a parent whose child had fallen off their bike. "Are you all okay?"

"Very much so," the Wongtok replied.

Tom motioned for the group to head into the kitchen. He gazed upon the Wongtoks who waddled their way from the hallway. "How did you learn our language?"

"Is it correct that your people have a system in space?" one of the Wongtoks asked, this being the first time that the boys heard another speak that wasn't their leader.

Matt nodded. "Yes, we do. It's called the International Space Station."

"It is through this device that we heard and leaned your language. The transmissions directed from there were received on board our now defunct craft."

"Well, this just gets better, doesn't it?" Chilvers chuckled.

The lead Wongtok tilted his head up, his eyes fixed into some distant memory. "And now, we will give you the dialogue you have been awaiting. Though I warn you, you may not like the tale that is about to be told."

"Oh, shit," Tom blurted out.

"What is it?"

"My Dad's home."

There was no mistaking the sound of a car pulling up on the driveway. Tom peered out of the window. "Shit, shit, shit, shit, shit. Everyone down to the basement, now!"

The car door closed. The footsteps made their way up the path.

"No time," Matt mumbled.

"What do we do?"

"What about them?"

"You're dad's here!"

"Everyone move!"

"Oh shit!"

"It's all over!"

"Not yet."

Six seconds later the key entered the front door and Tom's father walked through it.

A fairly average looking man, he was only a few inches taller than his son. He sported a clean shaven face and a terrible attempt to cover up his balding hair. He could have passed for a few years younger than his fifty-three years but the dark circles under his eyes gave him away, as did one too many laughter lines, betraying this otherwise youthful skin.

Richard put his coat on the stand and heard a cry from the kitchen.

"Hi, Dad, I'm in the kitchen. We've got some company."

Please let it be a girl, Richard thought.

Richard strode into the kitchen and was pleasantly surprised by the sight of his son and three very respectable looking boys.

"Well, hello there," Richard said with a broadening smile.

It occurred to Richard that although his son had had his friends over once or twice, he had never actually seen them in the flesh. His son and his friends were always locked away from natural daylight in his bedroom and they were always pausing DVD's looking for continuity errors in films. The fact they were sat around the kitchen table was a very refreshing intake indeed.

"I don't believe that we have been properly introduced," Richard remarked, indicating the boys. "It's very nice to meet you. I'm Richard."

There was no doubting that the geeks had impeccable manners and had been well raised by their respective parents. They all rose to their feet and went over to shake Richard's hand. *How very British,* he mused to himself.

"We've heard a lot about you," Chilvers said, trying not to wince at the tightness of Richard's hand shake. "Tom has told us all about your high profile business ventures."

"Oh, it's nothing really. Just office work I'm afraid. You young lads would find it all very tedious. Now, what brings you home so early?"

"Running club," Tom boomed, a little too loud.

"Running club? Really? You lads...can run?"

"Oh, yes. We're training for...um...a marathon?"

"My goodness, is this my son before me?" Richard mockingly gasped. "First you're socializing, now you're running a marathon, how marvellous! I'd love to hear all about it," an enthusiastic Richard beamed. "Why don't you boys stay for dinner?"

Tom, always one to seize an opportunity, jumped straight in. "I was hoping that my friends could also stay the night, if that's okay?"

"Well, of course it is. I believe your mother is making some of her world famous stew tonight."

"Great, I'm famished." Mark said, not really quite knowing why.

"Now then, if you'll excuse me, I shall need to clean myself up before dinner. I won't be long. You boys make yourselves at home. I'll be back down shortly." And with that, Richard was on his way to the upstairs bathroom.

Matt gave it a few moments. "That was close."

Chilvers waited till he heard the lock of the bathroom door "We've got to get them to the basement. Now!"

"Couldn't agree more," Tom replied. "Get them out of the cupboards and let's go!"

"I hid mine in the bin," Mark whistled with pride, as if for some reason the bin was the best hiding place for an alien being.

"Wonderful," Tom added sarcastically. "Now, go, go, quick!"

There was no 'go' about it, however. They didn't even get close.

Two words echoed from the front door.

"*I'm home*," came the cry of Tom's mother.

The boys froze and felt a punch to the chest.

They looked to the cupboards and... the bin.

"Let's hope they don't get bored easily," Chilvers stated.

This was going to be a very long evening.

*

Prague, Czech Republic.

Sofia had planned this night for two years now. She knew it was going to be the most terrifying moment of her life but Sofia's Grandmother had instilled in her a lifelong philosophy that love conquered all. So, after her shift finished out, she was going to propose. No turning back.

Sofia drove down to the local cinema where she and her love had met four years ago. They had been fifteen at the time and had instantly fallen hopelessly in love. And to defy their critics, they were now more in love than ever.

The pair had grown close over their geeky, mutual love of unconventional art house cinema. It felt like they were long lost souls who had always been destined to meet.

The young couple grew from friends into two people who were infatuated with each other and possessed something which some people waited a whole lifetime to discover; reciprocated love.

Still, to this day, they continued to bond over weird experimental films, films which sometimes only had a worldwide audience of a few dozen. But they didn't care. They liked what they liked and no one was going to tell them any different. It helped that Sofia's, hopefully, future fiancée worked at the local cinema house and they were able to experience unconventional directors and storytellers defy social convention with their off-the-wall-pictures.

Sofia pulled up and walked inside the movie theatre. She eyed her love and walked up to the ticket desk.

"Hi."

"Hi."

Sofia took a breath, swallowed hard and took to one knee, and slowly produced a ring. It wasn't the most expensive one in the jewellers but it was all Sofia could afford. She sensed what felt like hundreds of eyes watching her, each as hopeful as she was.

"Will…hm…what I mean…you…me…will…will you marry me?"

A pause lingered for what felt like an eternity.

Then….

"Yes, I will," she replied.

The crowd erupted with applause and whistles as Sofia raced up to embrace her fiancée.

"I love you," Sofia said.

"I love you, too," Milena replied.

The two girls on the edge of a new life together kissed like the world around them didn't exist. They celebrated their engagement the only way they knew how; they took to screen 5 of the picture house and settled down to watch the latest non-mainstream offering.

They wrapped their fingers into each other's hands and knew only that their love was real and that was all that they needed.

Soon would come the planning of a very geeky wedding. They couldn't wait, for they were in love.

*

A few hours later and the dinner table was set for a lavish feast. Richard had pulled a few extra chairs from the shed and his loving wife, Carol, had generously cooked more than was needed. One chair was left vacant, due to be filled by Tom's sister in a little while who was unexpectedly on her way home from university. Meanwhile, Carol was making notes in her head as to what she could serve for dessert.

Carol looked every bit the doting mother and wife, still slim for her fifty-one years and she came complete with a friendly smile that could melt the iciest of hearts. She whirled around the kitchen like an Olympic ice skater and served giant helpings of stew onto welcoming plates and growling stomachs. Carol could have sworn there were more than three extra guests with the rumbling of aching stomachs but she threw herself into entertaining her son's friends with gusto and she promised herself she would not be distracted by anything.

Carol thrived in the kitchen and loved entertaining. She came alive most during the Christmas season, or to be more precise, Carol began her preparations for the big day in mid-September. She burned the midnight oil at both ends until the twenty-fifth of December, when finally, after the turkey had been served and eaten, Carol went into a semi-coma on the couch until New Year's Eve. Richard and Tom had never understood why she did it but she loved caring for her family so they were happy to let her do it.

The geeks, though hungry and a little fatigued, were just grateful that none of Carol's ingredients had been needed from a *certain* few cupboards. Any minute now, they expected that she would open a door to find a little Wongtok sat on top of the baked beans.

Once everyone was sorted with dinner, Carol finally served her own food then sat down to eat.

Chilvers was becoming a little concerned that Tom's mother never seemed to stop smiling and he was intrigued as to whether she could eat with that slightly creepy '*1950's American Housewife*' grin that she bore so well. After a few moments, his worst fears were realised.

"So, what did you boys get up to at school today then?" Carol pleasantly questioned, her blinding white teeth beaming through half chewed stew.

"Well," Tom said. "We had geography first. Very dull."

As Chilvers was about to concoct a story of an average day at school, he turned to his left to the sound of a violent heaving sound erupting from Mark's mouth.

"Young man, are you alright?" Carol questioned.

"I'd rather not answer that to be honest," he managed over the sound of more gut wrenching heaving. Matt noted that Mark was on the verge of spewing up entirely.

"No, please, you don't look very well," Carol probed further.

"Honestly, I don't think I can answer just yet as I'm trying to digest this God forsaken stew."

An awkward silence hung in the air.

While everyone registered the offence and rudeness of Mark's comment, it took the culprit himself a moment to realise what he'd said. When the light bulb turned on, Mark offered an apologetic smile.

Time for Chilvers to salvage the situation. "What he meant to say was that…he…"

"No, no, not at all," Carol quipped, straightening her back and making her smile so wide her cheeks actually seemed to be in pain. "It's refreshing to find a young man so honest. That is a wonderful quality to have. Never lose that. If you would like something else Mark, then perhaps I can rustle something up?"

"Good God, no!" Mark pleaded, holding his stomach. "My insides are teetering on the edge of civil war."

"Oh…I see. Well, just give me a little nudge if you would like something," replied the offended cook, determined not to let it show.

All of the boys then felt the sheer horror as Richard rose from his chair after declaring that he needed a soft drink. Richard went to make his way to the fridge but Carol quickly corrected him. "Oh, Richard," she cried out with a sound of genuine terror. "I've just thought. I forgot to put more cans of pop in the fridge. There'll be none cold. You'll have to get some from the cupboard." She turned to the boys. "I'm so sorry boys. The pop will be warm. Perhaps we can stick some in the freezer for a few moments?"

Richard changed the course of his direction. The boys gasped as they realised which cupboard his hand was reaching for. Their blue friends were about to be found.

Chilvers had nothing to offer. Matt covered his eyes and Mark clearly had not the faintest idea what was going on as he was still clutching his sides in agony from what was quite possibly the worst served food he'd ever tasted. Luckily, Tom stepped up to the plate.

"Father!" he screamed with sheer aggression that was a little too much, though he quickly changed his tone to a calmer one. "You have had a hard day of... *business*, why don't you sit down and I'll pour some drinks for us all."

With his finger touching the cupboard handle, Richard smiled at his son's gesture and nodded. "Very well. Thank you, son. My, my, your manners are on form tonight."

Richard went back to his seat as Tom bolted to the cupboard door. He opened it to gaze upon the anxious face of a little Wongtok who handed him all the cans of pop from the shelf. With nothing left to hide behind, Tom and Wongtok took in a deep breath as they both hoped that Carol or Richard didn't feel any other need to venture to the unit.

"Bet the drinks taste like cat piss," Mark murmured to himself, earning a glare off Chilvers.

Thankfully, Carol didn't seem to hear Mark's comment, instead, however, she was about to do something far more terrifying.

"I think this stew needs a little more seasoning," she announced, rising from her seat and gliding towards the far corner cabinet.

A cabinet that was most probably harbouring an alien.

"Wait, mother!" Tom shrieked. His brain searched for something, anything.... *He had it.* "Mother, have you seen Mark's skills as...a...um...river dancer?"

"River dancer?!"

"What?!"

"You mean like Michael Footloose?!"

"Am I?!"

"Oh, yes," Tom grinned, still unsure where exactly this distraction was going. He had to think on his feet whist at the same time getting his mother off hers. He pushed her down onto her buttocks and just spoke whatever came to his mind. "Mark recently won a river dancing competition. He beat off a lot of other tubby little movers. One of the judges said that Mark moved around the stage like an *'overweight orang-utan on acid.'*"

"Oh, I see," a gobsmacked Carol remarked. "What a... bizarre...compliment. I mean it's a little backhanded but you take what you can get these days, eh?"

"Well, we'd love to see it," an equally bemused yet joyous Richard added.

Chilvers followed the plan and so far, it seemed to have distracted Tom's mother from further need for her garnishing.

Chilvers motioned to Matt to find some music on his phone. *Anything to keep the ruse going.* "Mark has had offers to go professional. He has performed at all the... um...local school halls."

Mark, perplexed like never before, was just happy not to be eating the bile tasting stew that he was being force fed.

Tom arrowed his head over the cupboard until Mark finally got the hint that that's where the Wongtoks were hiding.

"Brace yourselves, for the performance of a lifetime," Mark declared. He then continued to do some very questionable stretches which in turn morphed into some ghastly lunges.

The stage was set and the wheels were in motion. There was no turning back. With all eyes on Mark, his audience waited with great anticipation. Matt hit the play button on his phone and so it began.

Mark stormed about the kitchen doing his best interpretation of the 'River Dance' whilst at the same time managing to look like an arthritic pensioner who was about to have sex for the first time in ten years. Richard and Carol simply gawped in horror at the hideous movements that Mark's body was contorting itself into.

Carol leaned over to whisper in her husband's ear. "I don't remember river dancing looking like this."

"It looks like he's having a stroke," Richard whispered back.

Once the little 'show' was over, an out-of-breathe river dancing protégé took a bow, only to be greeted by some very hollow applause.

"My, oh my," Carol managed to get out. "I didn't know people could move like that. Tell me, Mark, does dancing run in your family?"

"It's a natural gift," Mark replied, apparently having found his new calling in life.

"Well, I thought that was simply fantastic," Richard proclaimed, lying through his teeth. "Good for you for not letting a lack of talent stand in your way." It was the cold hard truth but now Richard wanted to briskly move the conversation on. "So, how come you boys were out of school early?"

Carol raised an eyebrow. "Really? Shelia didn't mention anything today when I saw her. Surely her daughter would have mentioned something."

Matt offered a shy shrug. "Oh, it was only an hour. They finished us early for...teacher training."

"Surely, they should have had the training by the time they got the job," Richard scoffed.

"Time is of the essence," came a voice.

"What the devil was that?" Richard quizzed as he stood up.

"Oh, sorry," Matt said. "That was me. I like to do funny voices...I'm working on a new character for a play."

"A play? Really? Well, you truly are all rare and unique individuals," Richard said.

The front door clicked open, then clicked shut.

Everyone turned to see Tom's sister walk in with a face that was unquestionably a vision of beauty. Holly was twenty-one and today had opted for a mini skirt and low cut top. While Matt and Chilvers had their tongues set to wag, Mark opted for a more vocal appreciation of the goddess before him.

"Well, twist my nipples and call me a pervert," he blurted out, unable to take his eyes off the female before him.

Chilvers quickly gave Mark a clout round the ear and then shot him a deathly look as if to say *'close-your-gob-before-I-close-it-for-you.'*

"I would like to engage in nocturnal activities with her involving a spatula and a jar of chocolate spread." Mark had a way of using his outside voice whilst he was inside. Chilvers had often wondered if he suffered from turrets. Normally, the boys had only themselves for company, this time; however, he had gone too far.

Carol's face grew with fury. "What did you just say young man?!"

"I'm just saying what we're all thinking." Somehow, Mark was still blissfully unaware of the implications of his words.

"For God's sake, be quiet," Matt whispered with an intentionally forceful tone.

The normally placid Richard eyed Mark with pure, violent disgust. He went to speak but instead he calmed himself and motioned to his mortified daughter to take a seat.

"Right," Carol began. "Let's all just be calm and try to finish our dinner."

Silence.

A very long silence.

After a moment, Holly pushed her plate away.

"Darling, what's the matter? You haven't even touched your dinner?"

"Probably for the best," Mark said, followed by a look of pain from everyone else. "So, Holly, how are you?" he continued. "Have you ever kissed a boy who still eats baby food? Packed with protein for my muscles." On cue, Mark began to flex his flabby arm, with not a hint of muscle in sight.

"Oh my God," Holly cried out. "It's hideous."

Richard slammed his knife and fork down, his face red raw with rage. "One more word from you and I will…"

"Dad, please," Holly interrupted. "He's just obviously a little slow."

"I'm just no good in social situations," Mark pleaded. "I can't function in them and just say whatever's on my mind."

"Oh, yes," Tom interjected. "It's a mental condition."

More silence.

A very, very long silence.

No one looked up. No one ate. No one moved.

Then there was a *click*.

Followed by a flash.

Followed by another flash.

Everyone slowly turned around to see that Mark was unsuccessfully trying to conceal his phone. In the seconds that followed, it became abundantly clear that Mark was taking pictures of Holly's cleavage.

The whole table leapt to their feet.

"Mark!"

"Holly!"

"Dad!"

"Carol!"

"Mark!"

As Mark heard his name being called with a tone of aggression behind it, he looked up to the Heaven's to ask for help but the sight that greeted him was far from Heavenly.

"Wongtok!" he cried.

A small bundle of blue mass had tumbled out of the kitchen lampshade and was heading straight for the pot of stew.

Chilvers just said it. "Oh, shit."

The boys exchanged worrisome looks, all tinged with a side order of horror as the Wongtok alien landed with a thud in the pot.

There was no hiding it now, the truth was there for all to see.

Carol, Richard and Holly had their eyes fixed on the pot of stew as a tiny blue being pulled itself out of the pot and then rolled over onto the kitchen table.

"Good God," Carol yelped. "What the buggering hell is that?"

The little alien sat on its bottom and began coughing up the stew it had swallowed.

"What in the world is going on?!" Richard demanded.

"We can explain," Tom said, having no idea what he was going to say.

"Yes, I think you better."

"I think…I think…" Carol stammered, closing her eyes. "What is this creature? Be quick with the answers boys!"

"We…we…" Chilvers tried.

The boys didn't have to say anything though. Actions speak louder than words and the little Wongtoks must have sensed the predicament the boys were in.

As if it had been rehearsed, the remaining Wongtoks all came out from their respective hiding places and crawled up to the kitchen table. They all stood in unison, lowered their heads and in what seemed like a non-threatening gesture; they held their tiny palms up.

"I don't believe it," Richard gasped. "What are these things?"

"Well," Matt muttered, trying his hardest. "These are…"

"We are the Wongtoks," a tiny voice said.

"Fuck me, they can fucking talk!" Holly wailed

"The Wongtoks?" Carol murmured. "Are…are they Chinese?"

Richard stood in disbelief while his wife clutched at his shoulder to keep herself steady on her feet. The boys watched their new found alien allies as they roamed about the kitchen table.

"We are an alien race seeking refuge on this planet. My fellow survivors and I cannot stress enough the implications of what is about to follow. Unfortunately, we must label time as our enemy."

"What are you going to do?" Tom questioned, a little hesitant to know the answer.

Without warning, the Wongtoks leapt up to Richard, Carol and Holly and flicked their fingers towards their eyes. It was all so quick that it was nothing more than a blur. Tom's family were then quickly on a crash course to the floor, however, the ever compassionate Wongtoks all leapt around with stunning agility to gently place their heads to the ground as to ensure that no one was hurt.

"Forgive us my new found friends. But now is the time. We must commute to your safe haven and there we will detail you of the information you seek. So, please, we must move now and we must move quickly."

And move they did.

CHAPTER EIGHT

8.51.pm.

It had been an interesting afternoon for Chilvers' Aunty Joanne. She'd taken herself off to the local boozer for a half-a-dozen or more cheeky afternoon snakebites and then she had invited some 'friends' round for a 'party with benefits'.

The whole affair had been going swimmingly until her unsuspecting nephew had called by. Joanne loved her nephew but secretly cursed at the no doubt expensive therapy sessions that were to follow in the years to come. And obviously there would be an interesting conversation to come with her sister also but that was for another time.

Now was the time to put her feet up, watch her soaps and annihilate a bottle of vodka. *Perhaps she could buy her nephew off?* Could be an idea, he still liked to play with toys despite being nearly an adult.

Joanne had tried to set her nephew up with a girl from the pub but he was having none of it. She was a lovely girl too, recently out of rehab and expecting her fourth child. *What wasn't to love about her?*

Anyway, Joanne wasn't one to dwell, whatever happened, happened and like most things in life, there wasn't a lot one could do about it.

Right now it was time for a Tuesday night *drinky-poo*, as she liked to call them.

No such luck. The doorbell rang.

"Oh, for God's sake," Joanne moaned. "Can't a girl numb the pain with alcohol in peace?"

She headed to the door, suspecting it was probably a neighbour nosing around or God forbid it was her nephew looking to talk about earlier. She didn't have it in her for that. Not tonight.

Joanne opened the door to reveal two, very fragile looking women standing on her door step. "Excuse me, dear," one of the women clucked. "Have you heard the good news?"

Joanne rolled her eyes. "Jehovah's!" she bemoaned. Joanne wasn't in the mood to converse about the ethics of religion and why her stance on being an atheist was one that she thought all should abide by. "I'm sorry," she asserted. "I'm going away in a few hours and I'm running short on time." It was a lie but anything to get them away.

With that, she closed the door and headed back to her couch and vodka.

Joanne never made it to the couch however; for she was hurled across the living room as the front door erupted in a convulsion of fire and flames. The explosion blew the door into tiny fragments, quickly allowing the house to become engulfed in a wave of fire.

Joanne managed to scramble to her knees, feeling that her pulsating head was pounding in undesirable pain. She wiped the blood from her eyes to try and make some semblance of the chaos before her.

The fire roared like a mythical beast from Satan's pit and through the blaze stepped the two, still fragile looking women.

"What the fuck," Joanne stormed.

The women stood in the cackling fire, the flames licking their skin but inflicting no pain. "They know that your blood kin is in possession of the fugitives. Tell them where they are."

Joanne didn't have time to process the unanswerable question nor did her raging mind make sense of the images to come.

As the fire danced around her body, slowly encompassing her with pain like never before, Joanne screamed in fear at what lay before her.

The last thing she saw was the sight of two elderly women's heads being decapitated by two monstrous beasts.

The last thing Joanne heard was her own blood curdling scream as the beasts ripped her in two, leaving her in the company of eternal nothingness.

The Xironets were hunting malevolently.

And they were close to finding their prey.

*

9.08.pm.

Darkness.

And then, slowly, one by one, candles began to illuminate the dusty dwelling until every crack and crevice was touched by light.

With Tom's family safely put to bed upstairs, Tom had taken it upon himself to find an old pair of baby monitors and placed one by their bedside table and one by his side so he could keep a check on them should the Wongtok's mystic power take a turn for the worse.

It was here and now, that the boys felt awash with a heart-warming sense of nostalgia. The four of them had spent countless hours as children in Tom's basement sheltered away from the already brooding reality of the world, of grown-up life.

It was here, in their downstairs lair, that they staged epic battles of good versus evil, of swashbuckling adventures of pirates and shoot-outs with cowboys and more importantly; heroic missions to planets beyond. It was here where their sparks of imaginations had burned so bright and continued to leave fingerprints on their lives to come. It was here that the boys had satisfied their undying need for adventure.

As the geeks found themselves witnessing time sweeping by so quickly, the basement of make-believe had then become the stage for teenage angst. While talk had still, and always would, remain on their passions and fantasy worlds, the boys had slowly started to notice the conversations of girls seeping in and of what they might one day do with their lives. And while they didn't like it, they felt the pull towards the future beckoning them to a new chapter in their lives.

Each of them, once in a while, would stop and reflect back on the love and laughter they had shared, and how sometimes, the shadows of seriousness and burdens of responsibility would weigh down on them greatly.

For now, though, the boys found the road ahead of them had turned in a new direction and every impulse told them to follow it. Fate had come a knocking and the geeks were happily going to answer it.

The chaos of the day seemed to fade for a few moments as the boys put the finishing touches to their makeshift den.

It was a new beginning.

A new adventure.

Each of the boys knew, deep down, that they were on the cusp on what could possibly be not only the defining moments of their young lives but also the defining moment of every human being on Earth.

What was about to transpire could possibly renew or destroy the very bedrock of modern civilisation.

No pressure then.

Chilvers arranged some pillows in a semi-circle, being careful not to put them too close to the naked flame; he had learned that lesson before.

Matt and Mark set about cutting up several cardboard boxes, making them into seats for their alien friends. They placed the cardboard chairs in-between each of the boys, making it an order of a Wongtok, geek, Wongtok, geek, etc.

Tom, meanwhile, was busy hanging a picture of Harrison Ford on the wall, hoping that their hero would inspire them. Tom gazed at the picture, wishing that if he could just ask Ford what should he do, then what would Ford reply? How could the boys deal with the exceptional circumstances they found themselves in?

As the boys heard the tiny pitter-patter of feet coming the down the basement stairs, their minds wondered to the extraordinary situation they found themselves in. Their head's collectively ached as the Wongtoks took to their seats.

In a quiet interlude, Chilvers couldn't help but stare at the tiny alien creatures and marvel at how each of them remarkably began to resemble the boys. It was almost as if the Wongtoks had unintentionally attached themselves to a particular geek, thus forming a connection like never before.

Everyone settled.

The atmosphere was soaked with anticipation. The Wongtoks were about explain their very presence on earth and the boys would be left to hang on their every word.

The blue beings bore a sombre, almost mournful look and it was at this moment that Chilvers felt his stomach tighten and twist, like seeing the face of a loved one bearing bad news. Chilvers, like the rest of his comrades, had gotten swept up in the excitement and magic of it all.

The magic of being able to hold a tie that belonged to Harrison Ford, of being sent home from school, of finding a space ship, of discovering new life on earth then eventually helping them seek refuge.

It had all happened so fast but now was a moment of pause. A moment to let reality take its bite. Chilvers let the thought drop that perhaps a bigger phenomenon was taking place far from here.

Perhaps their beautiful age of innocence was about to take a stand for its final curtain call.

"Is everything okay for you?" Matt asked, releasing everyone of their brief day dream.

The leader of the Wongtoks nodded. "Yes, thank you. Your compassion is an act of generosity that we can never repay."

Tom eyed the aliens. *They're stalling,* he thought. *They're scared of what they're about to tell us.*

The head of the Wongtoks sighed. "Our very being here has put you all in unprecedented danger." The alien couldn't even look the boys in the eye.

The comment caught them all off guard. They couldn't help but feel that at least the creature was being honest but it was still a difficult remark to digest.

One of the other beings stepped forward and began to pace. The weight of his words hung like the stench of death in the air. "We are being followed, pursued even, by our enemies. A race known as the Xironets."

Matt swallowed hard, his mouth suddenly devoid of moisture. "So, these enemies of yours…they know where you are? They know that you're hiding here on earth?"

The remorse that the Wongtoks felt was utterly palpable to behold. The leader simply turned his head up and winced, perhaps in emotional pain or perhaps in tension of pain to come.

"Yes," was all the alien replied.

So, the Wongtoks were bringing with them an alien invasion. They were being hunted by an apparently evil race.

113

There was only one question teetering on everyone's lips.

"Why?"

The Wongtoks smiled, though not out of happiness but because they simply didn't know what else to do.

The Wongtoks were mystic beings possessing supernatural powers that earth could only dream of and this was partly due to the fact that their home world was eons away, in the farthest reaches of the universe, where atoms were engineered through strange magic. The creatures also believed that some unseen power in the universe was guiding them, that this very force had brought them into the company of these teenage man children. It was in the Wongtoks beliefs that every living being in the universe was placed on a certain path, long before they came into fruition, and though that being may sway or become lost on the path, they would eventually find their way home.

It was time.

"Friends, please," one of the aliens announced. "Gather round."

"We will show how we came to be here, to be surrounding you now."

Tom raised an eyebrow. "You...you can show us?"

"Indeed we can."

The Wongtoks waddled into a circle formation, closing their eyes in the process.

"Take our hands."

Mark went to protest but Chilvers waved him off. Instead, he nodded towards the now calm beings and they all gently kneeled down, each sitting between an alien. Though the boys were weary of what was about to happen, it could be no more bizarre than the day they had experienced already.

The boys clasped hands with the aliens, noticing how warm and formidable their fingers seemed to be. The Wongtoks slowly began to chant, an undetectable tongue that was almost certainly gibberish to human ears. After a few moments, the chanting grew louder, slowly building momentum until its crescendo, where on a blinding white light erupted from the Wongtoks fingers.

The mass of pounding energy engulfed the basement as the boys were forced to shut their eyes, while the whole time the little aliens didn't break from their trance. Though their bodies stung against the energy, the geeks felt an innate, strong connection to the aliens like never before. Each of the teenagers felt the intensified feeling that they were basking in the melting rays of sunshine on a stunning summer's day.

It felt…blissful.

They opened their eyes.

They were in a realm that was not their own.

Blurred pictures became vivid imagery. The landscapes that surrounded them became tangible scenes that were real enough to touch, even though they knew they were not really there.

"This is our home," the lead Wongtok indicated, apparently from everywhere but seemingly from nowhere. *"Your bodies are where they were, it is merely your conscious selves that are here with us. You are in our thoughts, our feelings and right now, you are in our past. All Wongtoks are connected through their souls and now you have transcended with us. You have travelled into us. What you see now, is what we used to see. In a way you are in our memories…and this, before you, is our home world. It used to be our home world."*

The visions of the past in the boy's minds showed them visuals of astounding beauty, the likes of which they had never seen before. They gazed upon flowing rivers of crystal clear water, trickling its way through lush green hillsides. Exotic and wild plant life bloomed into existence with enthusiasm while alien beasts roamed the landscape, searching for nutrients. In the distance, the mellow, justified sunset seeped through the terrain, heightening the tear drops of every plant, weeping its morning dew.

"This is Zolandor. Our home. This is what it looked like over eight-hundred thousand years ago. At this time, only a handful of Xironets and Wongtoks existed. It was harmonious. Neither species knew what it was to be alive and so thus, we all learned.

"As generations passed over time, the Wongtoks and Xironets grew rapidly in numbers. It became clear that each race had a designated role in the balance of work and survival. The Xironets were naturally strong creatures; they provided the food and built shelter. It was a role well suited.

"The Wongtoks on the other hand, we discovered a unity with nature and so we grew into the spiritual role of Zolandor, tending to the balance of the world, conversing with cultivation in ways that the Xironets could not understand. We were a constant in keeping the flowing foundations of life at peace."

Before them, the picture drew dark and misty. Trees whittled away as decay and rot took hold and plants slowly burned into ashes to the ground.

Even the sky began to cry.

"The Xironets eventually grew restless. They constructed themselves a monastery. A temple of which they sought to teach themselves of a higher power, much

like the Wongtoks. Here, they decided, they would dictate and rule the world of Zolandor as they chose fit. The Wongtoks were considered weak and useless beings, worthy only of slavery.

"Our fathers and fathers before them were forced to mine for dying life, to seek and hunt livestock to feed the Xironets, only each time the Wongtoks took a life, their own life succeeded from them also.

"The Xironets found amusement in watching the death of their subordinate adversaries and soon tuned the hunting ritual into a game with wagers made of which Wongtok would die first.

"It stayed this way for centuries; even we were born into the iniquitous despotism.

"Then, three days ago...came the uprising."

The vision continued to play out in real time as the boys witnessed events unfold around them.

The alien's sorrowful voice continued his tale.

"It was my comrades and I who lead the resurgence. But it was here where we found something. Something that would alter the course of our history and our way of life.

"Deep in the dark cover of night, the four of us were able to break free of our shackles and chains and flee to a secret basecamp of our former village. Our elder, the sagacious ruler, the one who beheld all the powers and energy of life on Zolandor, had been taken prisoner for decades. If we could release him, then we knew that we might just have a chance to break free and bring salvation to our impoverished race.

"When we reached his prison though, we found that he was dying. He was starved of food, water and something far worse. The Xironets had longed to learn about the Wongtoks powers and had begun to harvest every ounce

117

of it from the leader. The King Xironet wanted it for himself, his final act to seize control of the planet and perhaps beyond.

"The dying elder told us that there was nothing we could do now to save him. Darkness would soon befall him. He told us to leave the planet as fast as we could, to go away and colonize new life on a new world and perhaps find some peace, some rebirth.

"We refused to go. It is not in our blood to leave a comrade behind. It was here that he told us his final wish. The elder Wongtok had deceived the King and placed all of his life's powers into a tiny crystal. He called it; The Aithēr. The crystal contained generations of knowledge and power, all of life's energy surged through it. Only the dying Wongtok and King Xironet were strong enough to consume its powers but if we could take it, we could then use it bring new life to another world.

"And then, like a star burning out, the elderly leader died. His grey, frail body withered before our eyes. We took The Aithēr and did the only thing we could do; we ran. We knew we must not let The King have it fall into his possession.

"It was then that we led the mission to free the slaves. One by one, we rid them each of their chains and instructed them to leave Zolandor. Our mission, however, was ill-fated. Around us, we watched as thousands of Wongtoks were slaughtered. The Xironets unleashed fire unto the world in an attempt to hinder the rogue Wongtoks. It was to be the planet's final hour.

"Though the urge to help our brothers and sisters was unstoppable, we had been entrusted with something, a mission, which we knew we must succeed in.

"We eyed a lone spacecraft in the distance and made our way towards it. Wongtoks fell by the wayside as they

struggled on. Not one of us thought that we would make it. The Xironets were decapitating our friends with such precision; it was inevitable that we would be caught. Word had travelled through the camps of our mission and our brothers and sisters wanted nothing more than for us to succeed, even if that meant scarifying themselves. As we touched the boarding ramp, it was then that we heard it.

"The Xironets had unleashed The Gehenna. A cataclysmic device that once triggered could not be stopped. The King knew we had The Aithēr and so, it was his wish to punish us. To stop us with every ounce of strength he had. The Gehenna was let loose, imploding the world into itself. The Xironets took to their ship, the Bloodliner, and as we fired up the engines of our stolen craft, the last image we saw was that of our once peaceful home. It was the sight of our planet encompassing itself with death and destruction.

"We do not know if any other Wongtoks survived. We believe we may be the only ones. And now, The Xironets are coming to your home, as our world is nothing more than a raindrop in the ocean."

The geeks felt their stomachs turn and their heads whirl as a thumping jolt rocked their bodies.

They steadied themselves.

They opened their eyes.

They were back in Tom's basement, though they had physically never actually left.

The lead Wongtok's eyes glistened. "We are responsible for the death of our race. We will not allow the same to happen to yours."

Tom placed his hand on the alien's back, an offering of comfort and friendship. "The death of your people is not your cross to bear."

Another Wongtok stepped forward. "Now is not the time for mourning. We must save your world. The Xironets will be coming here, not only on the hunt for us and The Aithēr, but for Earth itself. The Xironets will try and exterminate your population and take refuge here. If that happens, it is our doing and we will do everything in our power to try and prevent it. But it may not be enough. You boys will need to alert your armies and prepare for invasion."

"They won't listen to us, we're just kids," Matt doubted.

"And they will not listen to us either, we are alien beings. I have no doubt that they will consider us a threat and attempt to capture us."

"What do we do then?" Mark asked.

"In truth…I do not know…yet."

The Wongtok that had attached himself to Mark slowly rose. "There is one way."

All eyes fixated on the blue creature. Even his fellow Wongtoks gave him a quizzical look. "The key…I believe…is The Aithēr. It will be too powerful for one bearer, other than The King, and so the one who consumes it would ultimately demise. There would, however, be a short window of opportunity. In that time, the holder of the crystal's energy could wield the power as they see fit, ultimately eradicating the Xironets and their threat to the safety of the universe."

Chilvers shifted nervously, a bead of sweat protruding from his forehead. "But…that's suicide!?"

The Wongtok nodded, confirming what they already knew. "It is, but it is the only way. This is a sacrifice that we are willing to make. There is nothing left for us now."

One of the other beings clasped his tiny palms together. "It will work, you must trust us. While we get up to the

Xironets ship, they will have already unleashed their armies. That's where your people come in. You will have to fight them off, defend yourselves by any means necessary."

Matt began to look unsteady on his feet; he blinked hard, and then tried to speak, the words coming slowly. "I don't believe it. I…I don't know. I don't know what to say. We're not built for this. We're…teenagers…the government…the army…those people…those people should be talking about this…not us!"

"I'm afraid that fate has brought us this crossroads. You and you alone must choose as to whether you go forward or turn back around."

Anxiety flooded the basement.

This was now far from the cathartic experience it had been a few hours earlier.

At this point yesterday, the boys had been discussing how they might soon be facing a poignant goodbye to each other as they would soon be ending their tenure at high school and heading off towards different colleges.

That in itself had proven emotionally unsettling for their young minds to consider. They had never known any different to their lives thus far, they had only known each other. The prospect of not seeing each other every day had wreaked havoc on them last night when they were talking about which career each of them might want to pursue. They had lightened the mood though, as they always did, by reminiscing of the good times as kids and deciding that the future was not something that they needed to worry about just yet, instead they would enjoy themselves for what time they had left.

That was twenty-four hours ago, and now they not only faced the prospect of a changing world but the brutal fact that it could be ending altogether.

"My head hurts," Mark stated, rubbing his forehead.

The chief Wongtok smiled. "I imagine it does, Mark, I imagine it does."

Mark stopped short. "You know my name?"

"Of course we do. You are our friends. We have been listening to you."

Chilvers smiled. "I guess we are. So, you know our names...please, tell us yours."

"I'm afraid that they are inaudible in your language."

Tom shook his head. "Well, that just won't do. How about if we give you names? ...Or nicknames...they're popular in our culture."

The Wongtoks gathered together. "We would like that very much."

The boys stared in silence.

Matt raised a half smirk. "What do we call them then?"

"Good question," Chilvers replied, rubbing his chin. "Just the first thing that comes into your head, I suppose."

Matt knelt close to the Wongtok with whom he had become partnered with. "Gary," he piped.

"GARY?!" Chilvers blurted out. "FUCKING GARY?!"

"You said the first thing that came into my mind. That was the first name I thought of...Gary."

"Very well," Chilvers grumbled. "Gary it is." Chilvers motioned at Mark. "Your turn, buddy."

Mark smiled, something that always worried his friends. "I've already got something actually."

"Oh, God."

"Earlier when we were upstairs, I found some left over kebab and gave the little fellow some."

"And?" Tom coaxed.

"Kebab. I gave him some kebab. So...that's his name...kebab."

"Sweet Jesus, you cannot and will not call your Wongtok after a takeaway."

Too late. Mark's little pal had already begun to answer to the name.

"Fine, what the hell?" Chilvers sighed. "Kebab it is. Good God, what are we doing?"

Tom waved a hand. "Don't worry about it." He looked at the alien at his feet and smiled. "And you my friend," he said to the creature. "It's obvious what your name is... Harrison...or perhaps Harry?"

"That, I like," Chilvers proclaimed.

Tom glanced down at the last remaining Wongtok to be named and then to Chilvers. "It writes itself what nickname you should give, Chilvers," Tom stated. "Ford."

Chilvers burrowed his eyebrows, puzzling it over. Then, something at the back of the basement caught his eye. "No, I think I know what fits."

At the back of the musty basement lay a collection of old records and LP's. They probably belonged to Tom's Mum or Dad. There were some collector's items in there; The Rolling Stones, The Beatles, Bob Dylan, Eric Clapton but one in particular stood out from the rest. *Born To Run* by Bruce Springsteen.

"He's The Boss," Chilvers remarked, almost to himself. "As are you," he chimed to the leader of the Wongtoks. "Bruce. Your name is Bruce."

Tom's lips pursed into a broad smile. "Very well, it's sorted then. It is a pleasure to make your formal acquaintance, Gary, Harry, Kebab and Bruce."

Matt couldn't help but chuckle. "A rag tag group of misfit aliens for a misfit group of boys. Fate undoubtedly wanted this to happen."

A moment of light relief washed over the group. Chilvers couldn't help but notice that even the aliens seemed to laughing, if that's what it is was. Or perhaps his eyes were playing tricks on him. He suddenly felt an overwhelming flood of tiredness course through him.

"Come," Bruce Wongtok said. "It is time for you to rest."

"No, no," Tom protested. "There's too much to do."

"There is nothing you can do now," Harry Wongtok protested. "Please, take a few moments to rest. We will wake you when it is time."

"I don't think I could sleep," Mark cried through a hideous yawn.

"They're right," Chilvers concurred. "An hour or so is what we need."

"Very well," Bruce Wongtok stated. "We have work to do. If it is okay with you, we shall retire to the upstairs. We shall then reconvene at daybreak."

Before the Wongtoks had even made it out of the basement, Mark was slouched up the wall, eyes closed and gently snoring. Matt didn't fight it either; he threw some old newspapers off an ancient chair and settled down.

"Don't let me sleep for too long," he quietly mumbled, already half-asleep.

Chilvers and Tom extinguished every candle save for two. For a while, neither of them said anything. They seemed content to be in each other's company and gazed into the firelight of the candle, letting their thoughts drift wherever they wanted.

Occasionally, they heard the aliens above them speaking or shuffling around. Clearly they were working on something and Chilvers was more than happy to catch a brief moment of respite, to preserve some energy for the day that would follow.

"Can you believe what's happened today," Chilvers whispered, not wanting to wake the others.

"I know, I've pinched myself several times," Tom replied in a hushed tone. "It's been...I mean...you know what? I don't think there are any words for it."

"I know exactly how you feel."

"Who'd have thought it...aliens...aliens land on earth and they find us out."

"No matter how many times I've looked at them, it's felt like some kind of dream."

"It certainly isn't that," Tom concluded.

"You know," Chilvers began. "If you want to close your eyes for a while then I'll...keep guard or something."

"No, it's fine" Tom assured. "I think I'm going to stay up for a while."

"Tom, are you okay?"

"Yes, of course."

"Don't lie. You look...different."

"Honestly, I'm fine."

"I don't believe you. You look..."

"Sad," Tom whispered, almost to himself.

"Yeah. You look sad. Are you sure you're okay?"

"Don't you ever feel...like you've lost yourself already? Lost direction or lost sight of what matters... lost who you are inside. In your heart."

The brutal honestly of Tom's words caught Chilvers off guard. It took him a moment to regain his thoughts and throw a sentence together. "I...where's this come from?"

"Chilvers...can I tell you something?"

"Sure. Of course."

"I feel...lonely."

"Lonely? I don't understand. How can you feel lonely? You've got us! You have your friends. You've always had us. And your family. You'll always have them."

"No not like that. I mean…empty. I feel like something's missing but…I don't know what. It's hard to explain."

The genuine concern on Chilvers' face was plain to see. "Tom, go on, pal, talk."

Tom took a breath.

"It's always been there, I guess. It's like I'm aimlessly wondering through the dark…desperately trying to find any piece of light in my life so you can make a go of it.

"We used to have such dreams, such goals but now it feels like that has gotten away from us…well, away from me.

"Then these aliens…these fucking aliens came into our lives…and I finally had meaning again. Their arrival gave me purpose. I finally felt that, today, I was put on this lousy earth to do some good. I look around at the faces in the crowd, each of them uncertain of what it all really means. Thinking that they've finally figured it all out and then realising that what they thought was happiness is actually just an illusion. A temporary lull in the road on the highway to the end.

"Wouldn't life be better if we saw everything through the eyes of a child? I feel such a sense of loss when I look back on those days, we had such joy…and somehow I already know that I will never feel that joy again. It has already gone. My happiest days are now nothing more than a memory. They're gone, never to be seen again. And I don't like it. I'm scared of the future. I don't want it to come. I want to stay here, where it's safe.

"You know, I often think that, deep down, there is darkness inside all of us. For some people, they keep it at bay. They're good like that. They're strong. They're wise. For other people, the darkness appears only as a flash, never to be seen again. But then, for people like me, it swallows you. It takes you whole."

Tom eyes remained fixated upon the flame.

"But, you know what, after today, I feel like there's also a faint spark in all us. A fire in our hearts that lights the way through the shadows of night. I never thought I had it in me, but...now...now I do."

Tom caught himself, unaware that he had been spewing his inner most thoughts. He needn't have worried, however, as Chilvers lay fast asleep.

Tom felt some comfort in the fact that his friend hadn't heard his rambling monologue. Tom didn't even know where it had come from.

He looked around him.

The silence was haunting.

Yet...it was...comforting.

He allowed his body to relax.

"Our lives are defined by the choices that we make," he whispered softly to himself, closing his eyes to welcome sleep. "I think I've made mine."

PART III:

FATES FULFILLED

CHAPTER NINE

4.24.am.

The kettle boiled.

The spoon made its way to the mug then vigorously began to stir. Typically for the master of the house at 10 Downing Street, it was always the same; tea, black, one sugar. This morning, though, it was; coffee, black, five sugars. The staff, however, still poured the coffee into his favourite mug; *Mr. Grumpy*. The diet that he had been on for the past four weeks had most definitely been hurled out the window.

The owner of the mug was fully dressed at this early hour and was complete with shirt, tie, and his least favourite blazer/trousers combo. His thinning hair was showing prominent signs of greying, the lines on his face seemed to grow more visible with each passing month and underneath his semi-blood shot eyes sat two dark circles, as black as the early morning sky outside.

The Prime Minister of Great Britain sat by himself in his office. He knew he had only minutes, seconds even, before the eruption started. He had been awoken just over half an hour ago and briefed on the situation at hand. At first, thanks to his deep sleep, he thought he had been dreaming it or perhaps his staff were playing some kind of practical joke. He was confident, however, that he had most definitely heard the words; 'alien life' muttered to him. Those two words had been enough to rouse him from his pit.

And so it began.

Prime Minister Cedar Manvoid had become something of a laughing stock recently. His political party was revolting against him; he was even facing the motion of a vote of no confidence. He had lost his way on the world arena, constantly side-lined at meetings and events, even the people of his country had lost faith with him, his bills and testaments now openly mocked in media.

To throw gas onto the fire of his shambolic office, he had recently been involved in a sex scandal involving a Latvian male prostitute. Though nothing had been proven as of yet, the story had deeply harmed any chances he had to regain some stability in his party and save some of his wayward credibility.

Now, at this moment of crisis, Cedar hoped that his handling of this situation would firmly regain the trust of the people.

He was optimistic.

He was ready.

He inhaled deeply and braced himself.

Within seconds, the still office at 10 Downing Street erupted to life as officials from every sect of the government marched into the room and laid everything before the Prime Minister.

Cedar rolled his eyes. He wanted to go back to bed.

After a few minutes, the chaos slowly calmed.

"Okay, begin," Cedar said.

A slender woman in her late fifties stepped forward, with soft brown hair and a tightly woven face; she was Barbara Fisher, Secretary of State for Defence. She tipped her glasses to the bridge of her nose and twitched slowly, a nervous habit she had picked up from her time as a local M.P.

"Gentlemen," she shrieked, quickly shifting through heaps of documents. "We have reason to believe and strong intelligence to suggest that unidentified life has cemented itself on earth, more specifically; Great Britain."

"Bugger me," Cedar squeaked, and with so; a worrisome sigh from his cabinet.

Cedar felt his throat tighten. He fumbled for the right words but nothing was coming to mind. "Do…w-w-we… have any evidence?"

"Of course we have evidence, Cedar; we are not here on some pussy-footing whim!" Barbara shot back. She motioned to an aid. "We have over a dozen pieces of material, all of which has been thoroughly scanned and verified. Here, before your eyes now, are two pieces of film footage. Please play the tapes."

Cedar felt his cheeks flush as he shifted uncomfortably in his chair.

On the screen before them, the brief footage showed a semi-blurred image of what appeared to be four small creatures darting pass the camera. The beings were minuscule in height, almost child-like in appearance and had an aura of…blue around them. After a few seconds, they seemed to return towards to the camera. It was here that the image froze to the unmistakeable sight of an alien being.

Cedar clenched his jaw. "They seem…short…um… they appear to be…almost non-threatening…"

"For once," Barbara replied, "I have to agree with you Prime Minster." Though it was a half-hearted compliment, it was still spoken with an icy glare worthy enough to freeze water. "However, these creatures you are about to see…are not."

Cedar frowned, unsure of what he was about to witness.

The footage that then played out was a far cry to that shown previously. It depicted a seven-foot beast deep in dense woodland. At first, the whole scene was blurry, leaving the viewer to wonder what they were watching. Then, slowly, the monster shifted its weight to reveal its towering figure, an image of pure hell. In the claw of the brute, a small fox clung for dear life before its head came clean off in the fangs of the beast. Whoever had captured the footage, clearly terrified, cut the action short as running footsteps were heard pounding the foliage before the screen cut to black.

The office let out a collective gasp as shivers ran down the spine of each person present. Barbara turned the monitor off and turned to the Prime Minister.

"Dear God," Cedar uttered. "Is the person who took this footage still alive?"

"We don't know," Barbara countered. "We have people searching for them."

"So, what does this mean, Barbara? In short?"

"In short...we're fucked."

"I see," Cedar exclaimed. "Um, thank you...for your honesty. What is the next step?"

Barbara's loathing for Cedar grew with each passing moment. It was years of pent-up hatred that she bore, his ability to be utterly inept bore down on her soul and integrity. She had now had enough. "Permission to speak freely, Prime Minister?"

"Of course."

"You, Cedar Manvoid, are not capable of running this nation through this monumental and possible life-altering crisis. *In short?* I think you are a fucking idiot who should step down and let someone adequate and passionate take your position. That, however, would be a seismic move to make at such a volatile time when the country will need leadership most. Therefore, I suggest, that you become a face of safety and comfort but allow your bodying cabinet to make the choices that will so greatly affect all of our lives. If I would have had my way, you would have been out on the street years ago. But no, you refuse to go, clinging to this pathetic, shambolic life that you believe you have. Do I have my opinion understood, Cedar?"

Any other leader of a free nation would have felt their back bones stiffen like none other but Cedar Manvoid wasn't any other leader. He was a rat, a spineless, selfish rat. So, instead, he sighed. "Sure, fine, whatever you think is best."

This, in itself, only infuriated Barbara more, but still, it was the outcome she had wanted. "Very well, now, please welcome to the floor, Mr. Myers."

From out of the shadows stepped a man with whom he had recently been bestowed the title of Majestic Intelligence Officer. A made up title for a made up job as there had never been an alien arrival on earth before.

Myers looked tired, dishevelled even, as if he hadn't slept for a week. His shirt was rumpled and his eyes were distant. He was a far cry from the homely father image that he portrayed so easily. He was also a secret agent, leading a double life from the ones he loved.

"Gentlemen," he began. "I think that you are going to want to come to my home. There, I have my son and three of his friends. In my house, I also have four alien life-forms."

"I beg your pardon?"

"I am speaking the utmost truth. Four, tiny, unidentified life forms…are in my home. They made themselves known over my dinner table, and then they knocked me the fuck out. I woke up, no phone, no tablet, no nothing. I came straight here."

"So, you left? You left your house with aliens inside?"

"No," Richard said, his words pouring from his mouth with great remorse. "The alien beings were gone. My son is asleep in the basement. I panicked. I didn't know what else to do."

"Richard," Barbara gasped. "What-w-w-what is your plan-of-action?"

Richard rubbed his eyes. "My son," he proposed. "My son and his friends are the key. We must make them our top priority. We must go get my son."

CHAPTER TEN

05.13.am.

Eyelids opened.

How long had it been? An hour? An entire night?

Chilvers rubbed his face, shaking off the last remnants of a deep sleep. His head ached slightly, not surprising considering the day that had experienced.

The day? Yesterday?

Chilvers bolted upright from the floor and took in his surroundings. He was in Tom's basement. A place he thought had been in his dreams only a few minutes ago. But he was unquestionably sat in Tom's basement. Around the room lay burned down candle sticks and makeshift beds.

Dear God.

He jerked his head back to try and snap back into reality for a moment. If it hadn't been a dream then it could only mean that…?

"Wake up," he barked. "Wake up. Everyone get up! Now?"

Tom rose to attention instantly, worthy of a new cadet eager to please in the army. "What? What is it?"

"What do you think it is? We've got to go! Now!"

Tom, also apparently awakening from a deep sleep, swiftly got his feet and raced over to Matt and Mark. He shook them hard and screamed down their ears.

Chilvers wasted no time in making his way upstairs. The last he remembered he had been talking to Tom… then…then he must have just fallen asleep. He cursed himself, wondering what had happened while they had been down in the basement. His mind raced and tumbled a million miles an hour. He stopped, panting from the sprint.

What if the world had already ended? What if they were too late? What if they were the last people left on earth?

Chilvers ran towards the window and looked outside. Nothing.

The trees swayed. The birds chirped. The sun shone.

Behind him, his fellow geeks joined him.

Matt scanned the kitchen. "What's going on?"

"I don't know," Chilvers replied. "That's the problem."

"Go, everyone, go, check everywhere. Find the Wongtoks."

*

Balham, London.

Sleep had never been a necessity to James Lightbody. When he was a child, his parents had taken him into therapy to try and cure his insomnia but to no avail. In his teenage years, James had attempted to treat his sleep deprivation by taking up extreme athletics in hope to exhaust his body and force it to repair itself on a nightly basis.

Nothing.

Next came an endless stream of blue collar nightshift jobs to suit his sleeping pattern. Still, that did not work; he only found that he couldn't sleep during the day.

James knew he needed a job where he could grab just a few winks of shut eye as and when he needed it. So, by this defect, he went to university to study journalism. A decade later, he found himself working at the U.K's top news station. It had been a well-earned justification to a hard-worked career path.

Now, it suited him. He slept for short periods of time, only when his body called for it. His mind was always on, constantly thinking of the world and where he would find himself next. The cogs in his mind were forever turning, awaiting the next story of a lifetime.

At this precise moment, James was asleep but only lightly. All he needed to be roused was the sound of his phone.

It buzzed.

"Hello?"

"James?"

"Yes."

"It's Clive."

"What's up?"

"Get dressed. Get ready. Be here thirty minutes ago."

"That urgent?"

"Yeah."

"What am I covering?"

"The end of the world."

The line went dead.

"Huh."

*

The boys were growing anxious.

They found themselves outside in the early morning air, furrowing through Tom's garden.

Matt threw his hands onto his head. "They're gone. They're gone."

"I don't understand," Tom screamed. "I thought that they needed our help? Why would they go?"

Chilvers placed his hands on his hips, his trademark sign of a young man wise beyond his years, deep in thought. "Something happened. I just know it...there was..."

Tom's eyes drifted to the upstairs window. "My family. They're up there."

The boys ran to his parent's bedroom, searching for three, sleeping bodies. They found two. His mother and his sister were still under the spell of the Wongtoks' power.

"Where's my dad?" Tom whispered.

"You don't think the Wongtoks...you know?" Mark thought out loud.

Tom shook his head. "I don't think so...and besides... we trusted them?"

"But still?"

A door creaked.

It was downstairs.

Chilvers faced his friends. "Quietly," he whispered.

They slowly edged their way down the stairs, peering at any corner for a clue of some answers. They pushed the kitchen door open and there stood four little blue masses.

"Jesus Christ!"

The Wongtoks looked panicked stricken, an eminent sense of urgency drowning their eyes.

"What's happened?"

The Wongtok that had become known as Bruce lowered his head, unable to look at their human friends. "I am so sorry. We are so sorry."

Mark's hand began to sweat profusely, a nervous habit whenever he sensed danger. "I don't like the sound of this."

Chilvers instantly wanted the forthcoming minutes to be over. He could feel the air changing, a wave of anxiety washed over him. But still, they had come this far, whatever was about to come from round the corner they could only lift their heads upward and face it. "It's okay," Chilvers stated. "Whatever it is, it's okay."

The tiny form now known as Gary stepped forward. "At first we heard noise, we hid in one of your rooms, and the noise turned out to be footsteps. From out of the darkness, we could see that it was your father."

Tom didn't hide his perplexed feeling. "My dad?"

"That is correct. He quietly left the house, got into his transporting vehicle, and went away."

"Oh, um, well, perhaps he was scared and went to get help. He did witness alien life after all...and besides, didn't you wipe his memory."

"That's what we thought too. However, from the look on his face it appears that it may not have worked. I regret to inform, however, that that was not our full explanation. There is more."

"What do you mean?" Matt hesitated.

This time it was the turn of Harry Wongtok. "A little over your standard thirty-minutes ago, we received a distress call on our homing beacon."

"Your homing beacon?"

"Yes, from our ship. It began to light all over. It was transmitting a message...a message from fellow survivors of our home planet. Stragglers who were out in wild space, calling for help. They said they were looking for us."

The geeks felt a tiny glimmer of hope in their hearts.

Tom almost hugged one of the tiny creatures. "That's... that's...fantastic!"

Bruce Wongtok took the lead. "They...the messages were not real. They don't exist. It was a trap...set up by the Xironets. Their ship is here now, as we feared. Your world is on the brink of a war like no other. The Xironets cloaked a signal, knowing that we would answer it. They drew us out into the open. They rained fire down upon us. It has begun. It has begun."

The boys stood in disbelief. They were standing in Tom's kitchen. Nothing, apart from the Wongtoks, seemed out of the norm.

Mark, who grew paler by the minute, slowly backed toward the kitchen counter. He then reached over and grabbed the remote control. He flicked the T.V on.

Sure enough, as clear as day, each T.V station was exposing the news for all to see. The boys gawped in horror and confusion as the world around them seemed to have imploded. For every act of courage yesterday where they had tried desperately to keep the situation under control, it now all seemed worthless.

Mark flicked the switch, hopping channels, all showcasing the same news. As each station bore more bulletins, the geeks felt more mortified as the seconds ticked by.

'BREAKING NEWS: ALIEN ARRIVIAL ON EARTH: BLUE BEINGS WREAK HAVOK'

'BREAKING NEWS: UFO – UNIDENTIFIED NO MORE: ALIENS ARE HERE!'

'NEWS ALERT: MESSAGE FROM DOWNING STREET EXPECTED IN MINUTES'

'BREAKING: THE WORLD REACTS TO E.T IN ENGLAND'

'BREAKING NEWS: VATICAN EXPECTED TO ANNOUNCE EXODUS'

'NEWS ALERT: - ARE WE READY FOR ALIEN INVASION? – PUBLIC THINK NOT"

'NEWS ALERT: CHURCH OF ENGLAND REACTS – JESUS WON'T SAVE YOU!'

'BREAKING NEWS: PREPPERS REACT TO ALIEN ATTACK – TOLD YOU SO!'

'BREAKING: GERMANY SAY – THE BRITISH DESERVE IT'

'BREAKING NEWS: ALIENS ARRIVE – RUSSIA SAYS – YOU'RE ON YOUR OWN'

'NEWS ALERT – USA STATEMENT – WE'RE WITH YOU 100%'
'NEWS ALERT: THE FRENCH ON UFO IN UK – THE BRITISH BROUGHT IT ON THEMSELVES – NO SYMPATHY FROM FRENCH GOVERNMENT'
'HEADLINES – TOM CRUISE REACTS – THEY'VE COME TO TAKE ME HOME'
'NEWS ALERT: STATEMENT FROM BUCKINGHAM PALACE EXPECTED – STAY TUNED'

The sun had barely come up and it appeared that a darkened night was already calling out the world.

Matt hit the mute button, not wanting to hear any more. The boys turned to the chief Wongtok, Bruce, waiting, hoping, for an answer. The normally commanding and extrovert little being could now no longer bring his gaze from anywhere but the floor.

Mark felt his eyes moisten. "Will everything be okay?" When he spoke, he sounded like a lost child, witnessing a loved one passing away for the first time.

The Wongtoks didn't move, not even an inch. Chilvers felt the need to say something, anything. "I don't know, I don't know if everything will be okay. I doubt it will."

The Wongtoks still weren't saying anything. When the boys needed their guidance most, they were just …standing there.

Tom, clearly agitated, frowned heavily upon the blue beings. "What's wrong," he asked them. "Do you feel responsible for bringing this…this…horror to our planet? If that's the case my alien friends, then don't feel any ounce of shame. The people on this world have been killing themselves for decades.

"A dying climate, endless wars, constant mistrust and bitter disappointments. We have lost our way, refusing to learn from the mistakes of the past. We have become complacent to allow the next generation to deal with the problems of today. We pass everything on to the next person.

"Failing that...we've...we've stopped believing. We don't believe anymore...in our futures, in each other, in ourselves. Now, I am telling you, this moment, this day, this is our chance to take it back. I believe that you came to this planet for a reason; I believe you came to save us... to save us from ourselves. Now, please, help us."

Chilvers couldn't help but feel his mouth forming into a lopsided smile. "That was...quite something," Chilvers beamed. "You ever consider going into politics?"

Matt burst out laughing, not because he found anything funny but simply because he didn't know what else to do. "You should stand in front of all the cameras in the world...and tell them that speech."

"I don't think I'd remember it," Tom smirked.

The Wongtoks tilted their heads. They each individually waddled over to Tom and patted his leg, one even purring as he hugged it.

Bruce Wongtok nodded to each of his comrades. "We will do everything in our power to help you. We...it...it looks like we had forgotten our place. Thank you for your reminding us."

Matt pointed to the silent T.V. "Look, something's happening." He grabbed the remote and turned the sound back up.

On the T.V screen before them; utter carnage played out.

A dark storm seemed to cover the screen. A reporter, James Lightbody, appeared to be dazed and confused as he held his hand to his ear piece, straining to hear his consultants speaking directly to him.

"We're live at the scene of history," James began, the nervousness clear in his voice, perhaps at the notion that he was covering the biggest story for a millennium. *"If you've just joined us, what I am about to say may shock and disturb you but we can now confirm that alien life forms are here on earth. I repeat once more, an unidentified alien specimen is here on earth and as far we know; it is exclusively here in England. We are being told that – wait, look up there!"*

The camera man tilted the angle skyward. Inch by inch, the sky grew dark as a gigantic spacecraft filled the heavens. The shrieks and screams of the gathered crowd filled the airwaves.

The boys and blue beings watched the drama unfold.

"Is that what I think it is?" Matt asked.

"Yes," Gary Wongtok replied. "It's the *Bloodliner.* It's the Xironets ship. They are preparing for invasion."

Chilvers didn't know which way to look. "We have to move. We have to get the Wongtoks to the government and tell them everything."

"He's right," Matt nodded. "They've no choice but to listen to you now."

The Wongtoks concurred till one looked up. "We haven't much time."

Tom froze, the blood draining from his face. He inched forward to the T.V set, squinting with each step. As his finger touched the screen, he picked up the control and pressed pause. He turned, aching with each movement. "Look," he uttered.

"At what?" Mark asked.

Tom felt time stand still. His eyes reflected to another place far from here. "Look at that man at the front of the crowd, the one with the army forces. That's...that's my dad."

*

Children screamed, parents panicked and bystanders dismayed.

The ship loomed large into view, hovering over what felt like the entire planet. Crowd members began to whisper at how this could possibly be happening and over such a quaint little English town.

The military swiftly began to bark orders at anyone who posed a risk. Over by one of the street corners, a news correspondent could be heard relaying his findings.

"We have word," James Lightbody announced. "We have word that Her Majesty the Queen has been taken into a secure lockdown. No one, I repeat, no one is to be on the streets. We are being told to stay inside and lock all windows and doors."

Richard had arrived at the scene a few minutes ago and quickly shook off the presence of the media. He hated them. They amalgamated every piece of truth into a work of pure fiction to suit their needs. They were beyond the lowest of the low, they were scum. Still, he knew very well that it was vital they be here to tell the British people to run for safety.

Richard swung around, his phone buzzing with a call from Downing Street. He reaffirmed to his second in command to continue the evacuation as quickly as possible.

He almost blocked the news correspondent out of his hearing altogether.

James Lightbody was desperately taking in the action before him whilst trying to get a cohesive sentence out of his crew back at HQ. "The United Nations are to be…" his words drifted off, trailing into the atmosphere.

"Fuck me, are you seeing this?"

Lightbody's camera did see it; for his angle was already gazing upwards and following the latest development.

From the heavens above emerged a second, smaller spaceship.

The crowd gasped.

Lightbody stood stunned.

Richard's fears heightened.

The Wongtoks battered little saucer prepared to land.

CHAPTER ELEVEN

The flying scrap piece of metal landed on the dirt ridden street grass bank with a definitive thud. Smoke evaporated into the morning sky whilst clumsy clunking sounds could be heard from the inside.

Soldiers raised their weapons while on-lookers, who should have known better than to be standing metres away from a spaceship, looked on as the opening hatch hissed and slowly creaked down, exposing the inner belly on the tiny ship.

One by one, four silhouettes appeared through the smoke. Tiny in height and small in stature, Richard raised his hand, readying the armed forces to open fire when needed.

Then, another shadow appeared on the ramp.

Tall, gangly...and human?

Then, a second humanoid shadow made itself known and then finally a third.

Richard held his command for a few moments longer, the moments themselves feeling like an eternity.

From the smoke emerged four tiny blue creatures. They walked slowly with their little palms held up in the air.

Behind them...Chilvers, Matt and Mark.

The puzzlement was outstanding.

Chilvers spotted Tom's dad and, well, didn't really quite know what to say. "Hello," seemed as good as start as any.

"What the fuck?" was all he replied.

Chilvers, who along with Matt and Mark held their hands in the air, motioned for the group to slowly edge towards the crowd and towards Richard.

"Hold your fire, keep aim," Richard barked. He extended his voice over to the geeks. "Boys, I don't know what this is but you need to BE CAREFUL. STOP RIGHT NOW!"

"You're going to want to hear us out," Chilvers shouted.

Richard stopped, his eyes viciously scanning the image in front of him. Then it hit him. Something was missing. "Where's my son?"

THRITEEN MINUTES AGO...

Overlooking Tom's back garden lay an unused wasteland of soil, rubbish and vermin. The council had been threatening to build more houses on the baron site for years but nothing had ever come to it.

That had been a stroke of luck, as the Wongtoks, fleeing from the trap the Xironets had set, were able to make another crash landing in their escape.

Once the boys had witnessed the revelations on the news that the world was on the brink of collapse, they hopped over the fence panels and made their way to the ship in hope of reaching the armed forces and government officials in time, in an attempt to try and salvage some of the situation.

The Wongtoks scampered up the opening hatch and could be heard firing up the ship.

As they reached the ship, however, Tom stopped short. "I can't come with you," he panicked.

"What do you mean?" Matt questioned, a little furious at Tom's cowardly act despite his rousing speech of courage only minutes ago.

"No, no," he frantically replied. "It's not like that, I've left something behind. I need to go get it and then I'll catch up with you."

Chilvers almost violently grabbed Tom's collar. "This is really not the time for games. We have to go. Now!"

Tom pulled away, vehemently protesting. "Look, do you think this is it? Is this the final stand?"

Mark simply nodded. "Well, yeah, probably."

"In that case, we better do it right. At least I can say I did the right thing." Tom looked to the ground, composing himself, then finally, back at his friends. "You have to trust me on this. It'll all make sense. Now, go!"

He didn't give them time to answer. He turned, climbed the fence back to his house and ran like an Olympic whippet.

"I don't know what's going through his head," Chilvers remarked. "But we need to go now if we've got even a fighting chance at this thing."

They climbed aboard the ship as it began to hover and they set course for the epicentre of what they most certainly knew would be the end of days.

PRESENT MOMENT...

Richard stood confused. "So...he went back to get something?"

Chilvers nodded. "Um, yes, that's all we know."

As the crowd watched on in stunned silence, from up above them, the Xironets ship generated a thunderous boom-like sound. The gathered spectators took to the floor as Richard feared that the attack had begun. From out of the corner of his eye, he saw a tiny creature gesture towards him.

"Please, if I may?" the being said.

"Oh, yes, that's right," Richard exclaimed. "You can talk."

"Fuck me," a lone voice cried from the crowd.

Bruce Wongtok wasted no time. "These human beings are our friends. They have helped us and now we are going to help you. That ship above you, that ship is here to capture us and exterminate your race. They are here to inhabit your world. Please, you must let us help you."

Silence.

Then a few whispers from the ever growing crowd. Even the soldiers had lowered their weapons to listen to this alien life form speak their own language.

Gradually, the whispers grew to cries.

"Bollocks to this," a voice cried. "They're fucking aliens!"

Like a supernova exploding into a hundred million particles, the crowd began to run in every direction possible. Armed forces struggled to contain the mass hysteria as men, women and children got caught in the stampede. Chilvers suppressed the urge that he himself should run. He knew he was here for a reason and he had to see it through.

Eventually, Richard found himself alone, facing the four creatures and three supposed saviours.

Matt carefully lowered his surrendering hands. "You need to let these beings explain what they are going to do. You need to assist them."

Richard's words came stern. "You are children in an adult world. Those creatures will be seized and we will take to fight with the incoming threat. I have no time for games."

"It's not a game," came a familiar voice. "You do not know what we've seen these past twenty-four hours."

Tom emerged through the grappling crowd. He looked sweaty and flushed from his apparent run from his home but he carried a new aura of confidence with him, a new determined face that his friends had never seen before.

From his shoulder hung a small satchel; shut tightly with a small padlock. "We have witnessed things that you could only imagine. You seemed to have kept a secret from me for a long time, this whole, *working for the government thing*; I think that buys me a little favour."

Words failed everyone.

Richard knew it was never going to be easy but he knew he had never wanted it to come to this. Time was ticking by and it seemed only to be accelerating without giving any pause for consideration.

Richard eyed the Wongtoks and then eyed his intelligence officer. "I'm sorry, son. I'm sorry."

Tom moved his mouth, hoping for words to find their way out. "Sorry for what?"

As if from nowhere, dozens of armoured-clad men swamped the Wongtoks and began to seize them into tiny cages. The tiny beings wailed out in agony as their bodies began to throb from their captors. Despite everything, however, they did not resist and showed no aggression as the enforcers were under brutal instruction to do what was necessary in order to keep the people safe.

What came next, however, Richard was not prepared for.

Officers moved in onto the boys. They wrestled them to the floor, attempting to detain them along with the Wongtoks. Despite their lack of strength and muscles, the boys put up a worthy enough struggle, resisting the enforcers at every move.

"Stop, stop," Richard cried. "That is my son, what are you doing?"

"We have direct orders," an officer stated. "I'm sorry, sir, but this goes above you."

"But they're just boys," Richard stammered out. "They're children; they have no part in this."

The officer hesitated. Richard seized the moment.

"Please," Richard pleaded. "Please, just give me a moment with them. Just a moment, that's all I ask."

The officer bit his lip. "One minute," he whispered. "That's all."

Richard moved closer to the boys but silently noted that a few officers in the not-too-far-distance still had their guns raised.

Tom felt the fire rise inside, if there was ever a moment, then *this was it*. The young son now stood before his father, a man with whom he barely now recognized. He fought back a tear, not wanting to show weakness, a strange thought considering what was swirling through his mind. "Dad, if you are ever going to trust someone then this is the moment. You've got to trust me right this very second."

Richard gripped his son tightly. "This is not a fantasy. This is not one of your silly games or science-fiction films. At any moment, we could all die. Look up above you! That thing, that monstrous ship could rain hell down upon us at any moment and I am trying to do my best to stop it. Within a few moments time, the Prime Minister will order the destruction of that ship by any means necessary. Do you know what that means, son, do you? Do any of you boys know what that means?"

Tom's gaze turned away from his father. "All I'm asking is for you to trust me."

Mark, whose face was pinned forcefully against the ground, spoke up from underneath the boot of an officer. "For once, I think you need to listen to your son."

Richard tightened his grip on his son's arm more than he would have liked to. "Just stop it," he growled. "Stop it! All of you!"

As if on cue, a deafening roar erupted from the skies above. An opening in the bottom of the Xironets ship presented itself, then, from the narrow hole, appeared a mechanical sphere, which in itself opened up. Then, for all to hear, a continuous humming whirled to life.

"What's happening?" Richard whispered.

From inside one of the now guarded cages, the chief Wongtok desperately shouted out. "It's charging itself. The ship is gaining enough power to unleash the firing torrent."

"So, it's a weapon?" Richard quizzed the alien, only a moment later realising that he was engaging in a dialogue with a strange creature.

"It is," the Wongtok replied. "And one that will destroy all life on earth. There is time, however, before the weapon is ready. I believe The King will first unleash his army of beasts to find us. That will be our opportunity to end them."

Richard's head pounded with a pain that he had never experienced before. Here he was, a man respected by the government for his intelligence and tenaciousness, and now he was taking ideas from a little creature that looked no bigger than an under-average height child.

Richard shook his head, hoping to clear his mind from drowning in conflicting thoughts. "So, you're saying we have a small window of opportunity to get up there and strike? Are you suggesting that our own weapons won't be strong enough to desecrate that ship? I find that hard to believe."

"Believe what you will," the Wongtok replied. "But I am not lying to you. The Xironets possess technology that you have never seen before. The only winning outcome for you and the only way I believe that this should happen is for a distraction to be created, and then, and only then, can my fellow Wongtoks and I be able to enter the ship and use The Aithēr to implode it."

Richard looked towards Tom, silently breaking him inside that his son couldn't bring himself to look back. Richard jerked his head. "Sergeant," he called out. "Release those beings at once."

The officers took their orders and freed the tiny Wongtoks from their prisons. Their tiny arms began to show signs of bruising, something that the boys felt a pang of pain for themselves.

Looking at his son and friends before him, Richard couldn't help but note how they had begun to transform into young men, standing tall with a glint of danger in their eyes. For now though, he had to put his personal feelings aside and take to saving the county, possibly the world.

Richard wasted no time. "So, you have a plan to get up there and end this. My son seems to vouch for you and I can't wait to hear the story of the past day or so, but I must confess that I am still uneasy about this whole thing. As I'm sure my bosses would be if they were to find out." Richard winked at his commander. "As I'm sure they won't…"

The commander nodded. "Understood, sir."

Tom stood by his father, sensing a small surge of pride take hold. "Theoretically, we can end this before it begins. It all hinges on the tiny crystal. The Wongtoks are going to self-destruct The Aithēr before the Xironets have a chance to get a hold of it. Our job is to make sure that doesn't happen."

"I understand," Richard nodded. He then fumbled for what to say next. "Getting them up to these aliens…I presume…there will not be…"

"It's too late," one of the Wongtoks interjected.

The group turned their attention upwards towards the sight of thousands of tiny pods being dispatched from the main hub of the Xironets ship.

"The invasion has begun."

Richard did not like the sound of those words. "How long do we have?"

"Not long."

Tom suddenly felt like a very small, insignificant cog in a mass machine. "Dad, what are you going to do?"

Richard paced quickly, heart sinking lower and lower with each Xironet pod being dispatched. He decided a new tact was needed. "Change of plan. I think I need to convene with some heads." He turned to his commanding officer. "Sergeant, take the boys, keep them safe. I must converse with the UN, hopefully with a little help from our friends here."

"Of course," Bruce Wongtok concurred.

Around them, it seemed that the sight of the Xironets descending onto the earth was finally enough to disperse the final onlookers. The geeks felt a knot in their stomach as they watched people capture footage on their phones at the onslaught of alien invaders descending upon them.

They felt uneasy at people gleefully capturing and sharing such moments of horror.

The boys had once taken a coach to Manchester for a school trip. They had been under the impression that it was some kind of museum trip for art or history or some kind of cultural metaphor.

In truth, they hadn't really been paying much attention to any of the trip announcements. They didn't read the information slip or bother going to the after school class in preparation, all they were bothered about was the fact that one of the teachers had mentioned that the pupils would have some 'free time' for two hours on the trip. The date of the school excursion had coincided with a book signing of one of their favourite actors who was doing a meet-and-greet at a nearby shopping mall.

On the morning of the trip, the boys rocked up at the school hall only to be met with horrific vision of all the pupils in sport's wear and hugging mammoth-sized gym bags.

They tried their damned hardest to get out of the trip, which they were to learn was a fitness boot camp of sorts but the teachers said that they had paid for their spot and the school wasn't going to lose that money.

So, the boys, against their wishes, reluctantly went to the sports day and after the five-hundred metre sprint, each of geeks felt like they were going into cardiac arrest. The boys had pleaded for the pain to stop but their teachers were clearly amused by the unholy sight of the geeks doing some physical activity.

Utterly exhausted by the day's workout, the boys made a pact with each other never to do any kind of strenuous exercise again. It was here that the boys decided it was too painful to walk to the bookstore to get their novels signed, so instead they were forced to sit out in the public area of the hotel where they were staying.

Outside, they had been greeted by the vision of a man standing on top of a building, his feet dangerously close to slipping off. It was obvious that the man was intending to jump; he was clearly just working up some kind of courage.

What mortified the boys most, however, was the fact that groups of passers-by had flocked to the bottom of the building and were taking pictures, then subsequently uploading them to social media.

The boys never saw how the scene finally played out, the teachers had gotten wind of what was happening and quickly ushered the boys inside. The event had stayed with the geeks for a few days, with Tom seemingly most disturbed by the sight of a man willing to end his life.

He had babbled on about for it days, even weeks after, desperate to know what had become of the man until finally he stopped talking about it altogether.

Now, the boys witnessed history repeating itself as people were willing to put themselves in harm's way, just to get a good picture and brag about it.

It suddenly dawned on the boys that they were being taken far from the action in a military jeep. Mark was the first to protest. "Shouldn't we be back there?"

"Absolutely," Chilvers agreed.

"I'm sure my dad just wants us to be safe," Tom offered.

"What are we going to do?" Matt questioned.

"We need to get back to my dad."

"What then? How are we going to help the Wongtoks?"

"Don't worry," Tom smirked. "I have a plan."

CHAPTER TWELVE

Cedar Manvoid was about to utter the five words that he had feared for so very long. As he did, the deep creases under his eyes thickened like mud.

"We are at war then," he uttered.

To his side, Barbara Fisher rolled her eyes. *Talk about stating the obvious,* she thought.

Barbara had given Cedar very clear instructions; she was running this operation and he was simply relaying them to the rest of the state heads. She quickly drafted up very clear notes for him to follow...that's if he could be trusted to read them. 'Stick to the script' she had told him for the umpteenth time a few minutes ago. Every time she looked at him, pure violent hatred swelled inside of her. *He really is a useless sack of shit. Don't fuck this up,* she kept repeating in her head. *Don't fuck this up.*

Whenever the word 'war' had been mentioned in recent times, it was usually referring to the 'war on terror' from a radical Islamic group or some kind of terrorist cell operating in the shadows. Today, however, the world was facing a war with an unknown species.

With Xironet pods being dispatched all around the world, it was vital that each country reach the same diplomatic conclusion, all with the same interests at heart; the safety of the people.

Cedar was speaking via a satellite T.V screen from his office at 10 Downing Street.

In fact, the leaders of the world were all speaking from their offices in their respective countries. Each leader looked as ill as the next and though sometimes some of them despised the sight of each other at these kinds of summits or emergency meetings, deep down each of them were happy to see each other, mainly out of hope that someone, anyone, had any inkling of an idea of what to do.

Naturally, as the aliens had landed there, all eyes of the world fell to Great Britain. Cedar hoped he was up to the challenge but he knew in his heart of hearts that all of his closest allies thought he was just as much a bumbling buffoon as the next.

From a makeshift military tent just outside the local fields of where the action was taking place, Richard was staring down at what felt like hundreds of monitors as he watched the leaders of the world converse and often bicker like school children over a toy.

Time was running out. The Pods were going to land on ground soil in what felt like only a matter of time.

Richard hoped that they would reach a resolution a little quicker than anticipated and he also knew that he would only get one chance to speak his mind and when he did; he'd have to make it count.

Just out of sight of the monitor that was focused on Richard, the four Wongtoks were quietly listening to the crisis meeting.

For reasons of his own, and reasons that were objected to by his staff, Richard had chosen to keep the Wongtoks out of sight from the rest of the world for the time being. It had been hard enough to convince himself of the prospect that he was taking orders from a little blue blob of mass, let alone bring them out and showcase them for all to see.

They would most definitely think that he had lost his mind and lose all trust in his ability to lead this mission. He also kept quiet that his son, his very own son, had been harbouring these specimens for twenty-four hours. The whole thing seemed more ludicrous as he mulled it over. The time for reflecting was later, now however, he turned his focus back to the monitors.

The U.S President removed her glasses from the tip of her nose and tapped the table with her pen, something that she only did when she was at her most fractured. Richard noted that the always shining and immaculate looking Jaqueline Eastmire was not wearing her trademark make-up or perfectly permed hair. Instead, she looked just like anyone else; tired and weary.

"It's obvious they're gonna stop at nothing," she bawled, her deep, rich Kentucky accent drawling the vowel sounds out to a never ending finish. "We have to put past differences aside and bind together as allies. The United States is the biggest goddamn superpower this world has and by God we are going to show it. We stand shoulder to shoulder with our British brothers and sisters."

"Thank you, Madame President," Cedar croaked.

"Even if I do think he's a goddamn pussy," Jaqueline scolded.

"Thank you, Madame President," Cedar repeated, not quite knowing why.

"Enough," The Australian Prime Minister piped. Here was a man in his late fifties but had the energy of a toddler who had accidently drunk gallons of coffee. He was known for his blunt, hard talking ways but had always retained a sense of humour. Today, however, his humour and warmth had been replaced by grim determination and eyes of steel. "We must fight fire with fire. It's the only language they'll understand. And you all must understand that I will protect my people at all costs."

Madame President rolled her eyes. *Damn Ozzies,* she thought. "Of course, all of us have our own nations safety at the forefront of our minds but what we need to do is to evaluate everything of what we know so goddamn far, and how best to use that knowledge to destroy these bastards before they wipe out the entire goddamn population. This bickering is pointless. Unless y'all don't have anything goddamn useful to say, then don't fucking say it. Next person, please."

The Indian President stroked his chin. Everyone had noted that he'd been poetically quiet during the whole conference but now he looked like he was ready to speak. "I am begging your pardon," he began, almost throwing the words away. "But it is clear that their war is with the west. I know that there is this whole 'Commonwealth business and all' but let's face it, no one is really taking note of that anymore. Thank you."

"I disagree," The Russian President piped in. He was a stocky man with thick, slicked black hair, who always wore sunglasses inside. He was a man whom few liked but yet were forced to deal with. Many noted that he always gave the distinct impression that he was always about to start his third vodka of the day. While he was wholeheartedly unlikeable, when he spoke, everyone listened. His voiced was slimy yet thick; the tension in his tone only accentuated his accent.

Richard silently cussed to himself. *Here we go,* he sighed in his head.

"Look," The Russian began, sinking his tongue heavily on the 'L'. "I am devastated to learn from my men that these alien pods have been spotted on our soil. Russia has a lot of tools at our disposal and we will do anything we can to help keep the world from ruin. It is my hoping that the rest of you will take my mind-set on this and not let personal ambitions get in the way of progressive thinking."

Not bad, Richard thought. Then he noticed the French president shifting about. *Oh, shit.*

"Let us dick around no longer," The portly Frenchman began. "I think it is time that certain '*weapons of mass-destruction'* made themselves known. The public will be expecting it. Any sign of weakness that we show these alien creatures is sure to be our undoing. While we squabble over details right now, we could have already launched a full scale attack. We are sitting on the very answer."

The president of Germany shifted closer to his monitor and waved a pen angrily at his screen. "Look," he began. "I have my forces waiting for my command and-"

His face instantly disappeared from the monitor. Blood hit the screen as the German president's head was decapitated by a monstrous claw.

Everyone recoiled at the sight and Richard felt a sudden twisting in his stomach. With the president's blood on the monitor restricting the view, the airwaves were instantaneously filled with blood curdling screams as the president of Germany's staff screeched out in horror as the Xironet devoured the remains of the body.

The image then cut to black as the transmission ended.

Cedar was the most visibly shaken by what he had just seen and began to sweat nervously like a school boy investigating the female anatomy for the first time.

Off to his side, Barbara Fisher sternly locked onto his eyes, silently telling him to remain calm and keep poised. 'Just carry on' she mouth to him, exaggerating the word 'on.'

Cedar clenched his fists in an attempt to stop them from shaking. In his top right desk drawer, Cedar kept a secret pack of cigarettes, menthol flavoured to allow the nicotine to seep into his system quicker. He toyed with the idea of lighting one, it might, after all, be his final chance to enjoy one last inhale and let the taste roll around his mouth.

He resisted the urge though. He had a better idea. On top of his desk, he had a small mug filled with bourbon.

That would take the edge off far quicker than a quick drag. Taking a breath, he chugged the remains of his spirit-filled mug and eyed the monitor that was aimed at him, and in doing so, he eyed the rest of his fellow world leaders.

"Enough, the time has come," he spat out with acid. "I know what must be done. Listen to me, all of you. We will not fight them. We will not go to war with these aliens; instead, we will do what Britain has done best for years...we will offer these aliens asylum and amnesty. We will integrate them into society and not probe them any further! I'm sure that, in time, we will learn to live side by side with these creatures. Who knows, it may be the dawning of a new era. Now, I beg you, open up your borders. It's the only way."

By the end of his nonsensical rabbling, Cedar had worked himself up into a hysterical fit. Some had to actually admire his little outburst as it was the most passionate they had seen the British prime minister in years.

Alas, he was, however, still a fool. A fool of which not to be trusted.

Cedar began to weep.

While no one knew quite what to say, Barbara Fisher absolutely did.

"Cedar..."

"Yes, Barbara?"

"Fuck off," she raged.

"Yes, Barbara," Cedar gurgled. "I'm sorry. I've been drinking. I'm sorry for how-"

"Cedar..."

"Yes, Barbara."

"Fuck! Off!"

"Yes, Barbara."

Barbara adjusted the chair so she could be seen by the monitor. She didn't hesitate in the slightest. "Barbara

Fisher," she stated. "Within the next two minutes, I want a plan of action formed and ready to be executed. Let's go."

Richard sensed his chance. He cleared his throat and adjusted his voice, making it sound more decisive and aggressive than he had ever tried to do before. "Leaders of the world," he regarded. "I believe I have the answer right here before me. Please, listen carefully and listen closely. May I present to the floor the informal leader of an alien race known as the Wongtoks." Richard turned his gaze down to his shoes. "Bruce, it's all yours. Take it away."

The leader of the Wongtok clan climbed up from where he was hiding and placed his little body on Richard's shoulder, making himself perfectly visible for all to see via the monitor screens.

Everyone was clearly shocked by the appearance of little Bruce Wongtok.

"Richard!" Barbara shrieked. "How long have you-"

"Barbara," Richard interjected, raising his palm up to the view screen. "Please, I've said my peace. I am asking you to just listen."

The chief Wongtok was by now adapted to human beings gasping and shrilling at the sight of his brothers and himself. He was, after all, a strange being to them. He was something new that he probably guessed a lot of the humans on earth thought that they would never see...ever.

Through the transmissions from the International Space Station, their technology had intercepted reports of 'life on other planets' but the Wongtoks assumed it meant bacteria or vegetation as forms of life, not he himself.

It was, after all, strange for him too. All he had known in his lifespan was being a slave to a ghastly race of Xironets and he had not known what these human beings would be like. He had, in hindsight, been pleasantly surprised. From the four young boys of whom he and his comrades had come to form a connection with, he had found them to be so selfless, so full of compassion and trust.

Everything the Xironets were not. The Wongtoks had most certainly felt the stars align to meet their new found friends.

As he stared down the leaders of this world at the monitors, he felt their collective emotions reach out and encompass him.

Bruce Wongtok felt their fear.

And it pained him.

The storm was brewing quicker than expected, however, and he knew he must put an end to their bickering and aimless indecisiveness. The father of one of his friends had already begun the introductions so Bruce Wongtok disposed of his own.

"Your world is on the brink of destruction," the little alien boomed with fierce intensity, seizing all attention from every monitor before him.

"The Xironets, the creatures that hover not far from your atmosphere, are here seeking something that my comrades and I possess. They are also here to annihilate your population and claim your earth as their own, as their own world died only three short days ago.

"The creatures took everything from us and they will take everything from you too. If, for some reason, I am wrong and they do not wipe out your population, then I fear they will do something far worse…they will enslave you, like they did us, and there will be no coming back from that. There will be no hope.

"These beasts are strong…they are fearless and they are ruthless. They will show no mercy in their actions and you must be prepared for that. They are also arrogant. And this, I believe, will be their undoing.

"My fellow beings and I have strong reason to believe that their leader, The King, is dying. What he needs is something that we possess, an ancient crystal that is the harbinger of life, a tiny fragment of our once tranquil home world, which, in the right hands could renew life for you on this planet.

"I personally will use this crystal, known to us as The Aithēr, and will destroy The King and thus eliminate the Xironets from existence.

"I have already secured the help from this country's forces and personal but we will need more. You must protect your world. I warn you, your weaponry and military will be overwhelmed. The Xironets have the combined strength of a hundred humans, while their weathered bodies are equipped to withhold the toughest of attacks.

"I believe that the secret to a victory will be numbers. The Xironets will expect your people to be submissive, to be absent minded and weak. You can overpower them.

"You must call your people to action. Call them to fight, call them to resist, call them to defend what is theirs. Now, please, I beg you, all of you, listen to me. Tell your people to do what they can. If the will of the people is strong, your world might, it just might, have a fighting chance of stopping it falling into alien hands.

"I understand that this must be hard to fathom, but I have already witnessed what the people are capable of and I can assure you, it is far greater than that of anything I have seen across the stars. Many of you may counter act me on that, and you may imply that I and my fellow Wongtoks have brought this here. For that, I extend my whole hearted regret. But the time for mourning and regrets must follow at a later time.

"Now, go, call your people. Tell them to be brave. I wish you all the fortune in your hearts. It is time. Now… now, is the time to rise."

Bruce Wongtok signalled for his fellow aliens to climb atop of a table that the monitors were placed on and there they stood, fire in the eyes and a determination to see through what they had started, to hopefully end what tragic horror they had brought unto this world.

As the view screens filled with faces of disbelief from each of the world leaders, to the side of the Wongtoks, Richard felt his spirit rise like a phoenix from the ashes. "Right," he began with clarity like never before. "You heard him. We know what needs to be done. It is time to fight. Begin the calls. Signal the people. Unite our nations and unite our world. Don't look back."

Richard saluted his chiefs, possibly for the last time.

"May God have mercy on our souls."

As the video screen flickered out, the ground violently shattered around them with volcanic cracks.

The Wongtoks eyed the vision in the distance, the sight of hundreds of Xironets pods landing to earth. From inside the pods, they heard the hideous screams of the beasts charging into the crowds, ripping apart any innocent before them in a desperate search for the Wongtoks and The Aithēr.

"We must move," Bruce Wongtok whispered. "It is time to die."

CHAPTER THIRTEEN

ELEVEN MINUTES LATER...

Every park was left unclaimed.

The streets were deserted.

The cities were left to the wondering ghosts.

Inside every home, every television set flickered to life with the forthcoming simulcast from around the world. Every parent clung close to their child, every sister to their brother, every lover to their partner, even the pets were held tightly.

If a lost soul had been walking alone down a street, they were welcomed into any home regardless of race, religion or any other bigoted reason human beings usually gave for not liking one another.

No one was to be alone in the final hour.

For the past five-minutes, every station had been brought to a standstill with a simple message displayed across a black screen;

'WORLD TO BE ADDRESSED IN UNITY – PLEASE STAND BY'

It had been decided that each leader would broadcast their deliverance to their respective nations in a live simulcast.

The words flickered out. The image flickered slightly and all that could be seen was an off-handed backstage view of a cameraman lining up his shot and ready to go.

The camera panned.

With anticipation fuelled by skyrocketing fear, the world watched with baited breath...

'SIMULTCAST WILL GO LIVE IN-'

'THREE'
'TWO'
'ONE'

*

"My friends," the Australian Prime Minister began, holding his nerve. If this was to be his final address, then he would remind his people just how invincible they really were.

"We are at war. But make no mistake…this will be the last time.

"Once this nightmare is over, we will forever find ourselves in a state of constant rebirth. Today, on our judgment day, the planet will be fighting not only for the freedom of today but for the freedom and for the lives of every generation that will come after us and thrive in our beautiful world."

He adjusted his tie, inhaled slightly and then stared defiantly down the camera.

"The people of Australia are a family and today we extend our arms and welcome the rest of the world to be our family. When families stay together, they are stronger than any other life force that the human spirit can understand. It is obvious-"

*

"That the enemy will show no mercy," continued the gaunt, frail looking man.

The Canadian Prime Minister looked tired in his eyes as he addressed the people of a country that he loved so dearly. Though the voice in his head was telling him the odds were against them, he could not show it. He took a sip of water and subtly wiped a tear from his eye. Not because he was afraid, but because this may the final time he spoke to the people of Canada, people whom he dared to call his brothers and sisters.

He swallowed hard and raised his head.

"These alien invaders will not stop until they reach their goal and they will not surrender. But…neither will we. What I am telling you may seem like some strange dream but there has never been a time when the world needs to be so alive. It is not only my hope, but also my faith, that we will emerge from the darkest depths of hell. We have –"

*

"…word from the white man that big bugs arrive from sky to kill us!" the hard-lived and weathered African tribal leader boomed across the plains.

All neighbouring tribes had been gathered to the epicentre of the village. The fellow clans had been surprised when the charity aid workers had summoned them to trek across the rivers to meet with the wise elders.

There, the relief workers had translated what was happening in the western world and what needed to be done here. At first, some of the children broke up in laughter, clearly thinking it was a game to be played. The adolescent members of the tribes had given a quizzical look to the white men and women but it was with the seasoned members of the tribe where the conversation had taken an unexpected turn.

To the surprise of the charity workers, when they had informed the elder leaders about the incoming alien invasion, they had not at all been shocked. It was almost as though they had sensed it was coming or that they had already been prepared for an attack for some time.

Was it...witchcraft? Or perhaps it really was a message from their devout 'Gods' above.

However the tribes had known about the attack, everyone at the aid centre was grateful for it and didn't ask any questions but simply accepted their blind faith, and in doing so, they took a little leap themselves. If someone didn't believe in God before, they certainly had converted within the last ten minutes.

Before them, the tribal leader shook his sacred talisman to the skies above them and held a small, wooden carved statue that looked remarkably like a Xironet.

"Today, white man our friend. We have to fight. Go... go get your wives to bring big pots! We use them to fight! Go...get lions to ride! Go get the elephants! Today... nature will take back what is hers! Go! Go! Summon our ancestors from the dead...we use them to fight!"

He stopped, only for a moment, and inhaled what seemed to be all the oxygen around him. He paused, and then began the chant. "We kill bugs! We kill bugs! We kill bugs!"

Satisfied that the tribes were now ready, he turned to one of his many, many wives for a brief, private moment. "My-"

*

"...fellow, Americans," The President began, her shoulders pressed back and the white, gleaming smile still lying underneath her grim exterior. Her aids had drafted a letter for her approval but Jaqueline had written her own. Her final words to the greatest country on earth would be that of her own, not some jumped up secretary.

Jaqueline had chosen to speak to the country from the steps outside the Whitehouse, not from the regular briefing room. This, she thought, would show an act of defiance, courage and strength to the world, which would ignite the fire in her people's hearts and let it shine bright.

"Alien invaders are going to strike all corners of the earth as they have picked a fight with us. Now, I know that you must agree with me in thinking that they have picked a fight with the wrong people. We will not be beaten. We will not back down. Today, we will stand together and we will stand tall.

"Like never before in the history of mankind, we are now called to defend our streets, our cities, our lives, ourselves and each other. There will be losses. That is inevitable. Though they may try and take us of our lives, they will never, ever take us of our hope.

"Sometimes, our world has never seen eye to eye. We have all suffered our share of demons and doubts but now we cast those fears aside as we hold the hands of our friends to show that the words 'giving up' do not appear in our dictionary. This is our time. These of our lives, these are our dreams and today is our day to cast our eyes to heavens and let God Almighty know that WE ARE NOT READY FOR HIM TO TAKE US YET!

"AMERICA HAS GOT A LOT MORE LEFT TO GIVE

"As a great philosopher once said: '*Friendship dances around the world, inviting us all awaken to recognition of happiness.*'

"Collectively, the world and our friends are about to walk through hell together but I assure y'all that we will wave goodbye to this shadow of evil and forever live in happiness. Gather what you can, join forces with whomever you can and join me in saying out loud…GOD BLESS THE UNITED STATES OF AMERICA!

"Now, hear me, when I say-"

*

"…people of Great Britain," came the calm, almost soothing voice of Her Majesty the Queen.

As the events had unfolded, The Queen had felt her soul renewed with a new, profound sense of sadness that she had not felt in years. Her material possessions now seemed like poor punchlines to comedians distasteful jokes as she had gawped in horror at the heartbreak playing our before her eyes.

She and her family had been taken to a top-secret lockdown safe house and Her Majesty had been duly informed that the Prime Minister was about to give an address to the people…*no chance.*

Not today.

Not on her watch.

She had ordered for a camera to be placed in her room then notified her staff to inform that whoever was in charge of media coverage at 10 Downing Street to inform the pitiful Cedar Manvoid to pull his speech and that she herself, The Queen of England, would address the people she adored so dearly.

Her most trusted advisors had quickly prepared a speech and handed her a piece of paper, a piece of paper that she had instantly thrown in the bin.

Over the years, the Queen had watched Great Britain become great no more. She had seen the pessimism and distrust in people's eyes. She had seen the spark of magic fade out until she was nothing more than a ten-minute address on Christmas Day. In the past, if Britain had proven one thing to the rest of the world, it was that the rest of the world had been proven wrong by Britain.

So, there she sat on a small chair in very simple clothing. A corgi sat either side of her, waiting for orders.

When the camera's red light had turned on, she addressed the nation and simply said what was in her heart.

Nothing pre-planned.

Nothing rehearsed.

Just the truth.

After all, that was what the British people had been denied of for so long.

Now, she was going to give it to them.

"Once again we find our great nation under attack. For years now, we have lived in the shadows and become a laughing stock to the rest of the world. We have always fought hard to preserve our great island and the principles that our ancestors worked hard to achieve.

"Today, we take those principles of greatness and love and personify them with each and every one of us who may have lost the faith. But no more!

"This is a call to arms; for today...we must fight. For too long, we have been left behind. For too long, we have lived afraid of the evil. For too long, we have kept our heads to the floor.

"Now, today, we look to the heavens at the start of a new revolution. I have seen that our love for one another is strong enough to move mountains, our love can ignite the stars above us on the darkest of nights, and today, I am asking you take that strength and fight for survival. We are the United Kingdom...and so, united we stand, united we fall and united we shall rise again.

"Make no mistake; I shall be joining you on the battle field today. So, no matter your age, no matter your ability, we must take Britain by the hand and lead her into the light. With every breath in my body, with all the hope in my soul, with all the courage in my heart, I am asking you to join me..."

One of the Queen's corgis' jumped up onto her lap and growled viciously at the camera. The Queen herself snarled with a flare of menace.

"Join me, as we take those aliens, and shit on their parade."

And just like that, within moments, the world was at war.

But she wasn't going down without a fight.

CHAPTER FOURTEEN

SEVEN MINUTES LATER...

Belfast, Northern Ireland.

These streets had been bloodied before.

Far too much spilt and for far too long, some may say.

Every crack in the stone had a story to tell.

Shankill Road had played home to an elongated war of territory for what some said still remained unresolved. If a tourist were to take a stroll down the stained pavements of this now infamous road, the marked walls surrounding them would bleed the history of a lifetime. Though the Troubles had long since cooled down and the legislations signed to declare an end to the conflict, the beliefs and principles of both nationalists and loyalist still rang out in the words they spoke.

Now, however, the streets were home to nothing but echoes. A piercing wind ruptured through the cracks and crevices of shop windows and locked up homes. Every few minutes, a dog bark could be heard in the distance, only agitating those who had barricaded themselves in from the oncoming attack.

Then, the noise came.

A noise in regimented unison.

It slowly grew louder and louder and louder.

For those scattered pairs of eyes brave enough to chance a peer out of their window curtains, they were greeted with the sight of hundreds of Xironet beasts marching down the baron, now dystopian Shankill Road.

The beasts had been given one simple order from their dying King; search and destroy. The Xironets were abundantly aware that if their King and Queen were to perish, then their own flames of life would burn out also.

The Xironets had studied the species of earth for as long as possible in the short amount of time that they had been aware that the fleeing Wongtoks had taken refuge on the planet. The alien army had been informed from their commanders that the people of the hospitable world would unlikely to be the kind to put up a resistance.

Humans were cowards but they needed to be dealt with accordingly.

The most cunning of the Xironet race had been instructed to find the Wongtoks while the remainder of the vast army was to complete the task of extermination.

The planet earth was to become home to the Xironets and nothing would stand in their way. The Xironets had an innate taste for flesh; their compulsive need to destroy would be adequately quenched with this, most likely their final conflict.

As the monsters continued their match towards the centre of the city, their grotesque nostrils flared at the stench of human prey.

Nothing would stop them. No snipers lay in wait. No shots rang out. No army arrived to defend the capitol.

But then it happened.

One lone voice above the noise.

A spark that started the fire.

An army of one standing in the face of sure defeat.

There he stood…heart pounding.

There he stood…panting and sweating.

There he stood…only eight years old.

Little Craig O'Conner took his place in the middle of Shankill Road with nothing more than a cricket bat for a weapon.

The Xironets scoffed at such a pathetic adversary standing in their way. The chase was on as to who would taste the little boy's blood first. As the beasts picked up the pace and leapt their gigantic clawed feet towards the child, their mouths salivated at the thought of the first kill. A small part of the Xironets wished the boy would run and flee, making the hunt and kill even sweeter...

...however, he didn't.

He did quite the opposite.

Little Craig cried out at the top of his lungs and swung his cricket bat in the air like an expert swordsman ready to battle the knights of old. As an army of hundreds charged at the child, they were stopped in their tracks by the sight of dozens and dozens of men and women bombarding the street from the homes.

An elderly man swept up the child into the arms of safety but still roared at the aliens and armed himself with a bladed weapon that was surely banned in most countries. The dozens of amateur fighters then became hundreds until it finally felt like the entire population of Belfast were taking a stand on the battlefield of their much loved home.

The Xironets didn't have time to react. Their human attackers wielded enough force and willpower to disarm the beasts and momentarily halt them in their assault. The Xironets were now impossibly outnumbered.

Off to one side, little Craig O'Conner flared his face in pride at his neighbours.

The human spirit was alive after all...all it needed was a little nudge.

*

The past minutes had been nothing but a blur to the geeks.

They had been swiftly taken from the battlefield into a very fancy jeep of some sort; at least the boys thought it was a jeep as they knew very little about cars. The driver had sped away at monumental speed around the streets as the sky turned a distinctive shade of coal black.

From there, they now found themselves entering what Richard had described as a 'safe house' of sorts. He promptly hurled them into the main room which was buzzing with military exertion and sergeants of all creeds and stature.

Richard signalled for one his men to come to the boys. "This is Officer Holloway."

"You lads can call me Chris," he assured them with a nod.

Richard's eyes darted to the window. "He'll take care of you. Do as he says and you'll be safe."

Tom was the first to protest. "Dad, we need to be back-"

"Enough," Richard snapped, waving his hand. "I have a duty to protect you. I have a duty to protect all of you. Can you imagine what your mother's would do to me if I let any harm fall upon you? I'd be crucified."

Chilvers opened his mouth to argue his point but that's as far as he got; opening his mouth.

"Not. Another. Word," Richard seethed. "I have to go; your alien friends need me."

Before anything more could be said, Richard was gone, leaving the boys in the company of the military.

"As you can imagine," Officer Holloway began. "We have much to do. If you lads wouldn't mind just waiting off to the side, I have a few things to sort and then I'll be with you. Anything you need? Water? Something like that?"

"No, it's fine, thank you," Matt said.

"Look," Tom interjected. "Officer...Chris...you seem like a decent bloke but you and I both know that the four of us should be out there. We're being utterly wasted inside this bloody safe house. We're wasting our time. Now, be a good sport, eh?"

"Sorry matey," Holloway asserted. "You heard your old man. My job is to keep you here and protect you. So, that's what I'm going to do."

With that, he gave the boys a concluding nod and retreated back to the principle computer screens.

With the world fighting for its survival just past the four walls they now found themselves in, the boys were allowed a few moments of reprieve as they couldn't have felt further from the action.

Wasn't that just the story of their lives though?

The boys were constantly looking in at the popular and the do-gooders, while they were always trapped outside the circle. With nothing to do but sit there and fester, the boys did just that.

Chilvers felt his mind swirling. He thought of the Wongtoks as he wondered if he would ever see them again or if they would be successful in their plan to destroy the Xironets. He thought of his parents and how the phone call he gave them earlier that morning might be the last time he heard their voices. And then, as he gazed upon the bruised and scarred faces of the people sat next to him, he thought of his friends.

In some ways, they were closer to him than his own family. He didn't very much care for many of them; they had never been a close family like some. He saw them occasionally at family birthdays or weddings but he realised that he knew very little about them. It didn't bother him though. The people he most cared about, aside from his parents, were sat beside him. His three fellow geeks were more than pals, buddies or mates; they were his true family.

From the blissful days of sword fighting each other with sticks, to the pain they had all felt when someone's loved one had passed away, they knew each other better than they knew themselves. If one of them was down or hurting, it was impossible for the others not to feel it. They were so tight with their bonds that it may have been improbable that someone could fit a gasp of air between them.

Chilvers wouldn't have had it any other way.

When it all was over, they knew that they could pick up the broken pieces and fit them back together perfectly, instantly getting back to the way things were. Back when they were innocent, back to a place where they truly belonged.

Chilvers couldn't help but wonder that if, for some unbeknown reason, they all survived this thing; then would everything still be the same in years or even decades to come? Surely the party had to end sometime. They would have to face the prospect of growing up, growing old and moving on.

Chilvers couldn't imagine a time when any of them would ever contemplate thinking about mortgages or job prospects or, Heaven forbid, cooking their own meals. And perhaps, if by some small miracle, each of them might find the perfect soul mate and start a new life of their own, becoming parents or protectors for a new generation. It was a world that seemed strange in his head but it was a world that was always going to be inevitable.

His heart tinged with a new found poignant sadness.

"You know," Chilvers pondered, his voice barely audible. "If this day is really to be our swan song, our final call, then…um…there are no other soldiers I'd rather have at my side as I ride into battle."

"Oh, cow me," Mark blurted out. "He's gone all poncey on us."

Matt felt his eyes go damp. "No, no," he whispered. "I get it. I do. It's like…I read this thing ages ago…I don't know where...it went 'God didn't make us brothers but it was fate that we are'...or something like that."

Tom wiped his eyes. "Don't get me going you soppy bastards."

"I think you're all being very over dramatic," Mark uttered.

Matt couldn't help but chuckle. "It doesn't really get more dramatic than the end of the fucking world you podgy moron!"

At that, none of them could supress a laugh. It might, after all, be the last chance they got.

The boys heard footsteps approaching.

It was Officer Holloway. "You lads okay?"

"As good as can be," Matt replied, probably speaking for all them.

"Are there any family members that you want me check up on? I'm responsible for-"

A thunderous roar erupted from the hallway followed by a thunderous *booming* sound

"They're here," the boys heard a voice cry. *"They've breached the-"*

The bellowing and unmistakable howls of the Xironets cocooned the airwaves as fallen soldiers wailed out in agony as they tore them limb from limb.

As the Xironets stormed what should have been a safe house, it was becoming more evident with every passing second that there was very little point in staying put.

Officer Holloway ushered the boys to their feet. "Quickly, all of you follow me."

The boys could only look away in horror, however, as the only place the officer was going was to meet his maker. A devilish Xironet arched his clawed fist from above and subsequently decapitated the officer's head, sending it rolling on the floor.

183

"OH SHIT!" Mark screamed out as blood spat itself all over his face.

As the Xironet moved in for the kill on the boys, it stopped suddenly and began to inhale through its nostrils.

"What's it doing?" Matt whispered.

"You don't think it can smell the Wongtoks, do you?" Tom offered.

"I think so," Chilvers gulped.

The almighty creature leapt to within touching distance of the boys and aimed directly for them. Seeking courage from deep within, Chilvers launched himself at the beast and was momentarily able to catch it off guard.

As the Xironet regained its footing, it stuck its claw right into Mark's leg, causing him to wail out in pain like never before.

As Chilvers jumped to the beast's torso in an attempt to knock it over, a mass of bullets rained from the corner of the room, inflicting wounds on the Xironet that it wasn't expecting.

The sergeant with the loaded gun moved in to pull Mark from the clutches of the monster but to no avail. With Mark firmly in hand, the Xironet hurled itself through a window and out onto the streets.

Chilvers steadied himself while the sergeant checked for wounds. "We have to get him back."

The boys wasted no time in pursuing their captive friend through the window and running straight into the maelstrom of war that played out before them.

*

Amsterdam, Netherlands.

The city of sin was under monumental attack.

As the armed forces did what they could to protect the innocent, the overpowering invading Xironets simply proved too much. Some of the local residents had taken to hiding in the canals to try and use the element of surprise to catch the hideous beasts off guard. The plan had seemed like a good one, but the Xironets soon crushed the brave down.

As the war around the city raged on, a decent number of the locals could be found in the coffee shops indulging in one final escape from reality. It was here that a twenty-something lad had come up with what he thought was a superb idea; to use what local resources Amsterdam had to offer.

He rallied what courageous souls he could find and ran as fast as their stumbling legs could carry them. Once there, the lad called upon a few of his 'acquaintances' and asked them to take their regular place underneath a bright red light.

His logic of thinking was simple; the alien attackers, like every living thing, obviously bred; therefore they must have had urges like any other species on earth.

To the surprise of everyone, not least the women in the windows, the plan worked. As the Xironets vision was temporally filled with that of a sin like no other, the locals struck the beasts from behind, inflicting killing blows to those monsters that didn't see it coming.

The Xironets soon realised the human's plan, however, and it wasn't long before the brutes gained the upper hand once more.

*

Tokyo, Japan.

Earth's vision of the future was now home to alien invasion.

At the beginning of the extermination, the native's way of life had been a crutch to them. The gigantic blinding screens and clustered density of the city had helped the locals gain some control of the war. Their futuristic technology had allowed the people of Japan to wield homemade weapons with stunning skill and ferocious vexation.

It was soon time to unleash Tokyo's best robots on their alien adversaries. The rest of the world hadn't really paid much attention to the development of their humanoid robotic colleagues but the truth of the matter was the fact that the development of these products was extremely far down the line.

As the robots battled with the Xironets, it wasn't too long before the beasts were pulling the androids limb from limb. It was then that the Xironets struck with force as the residents wept over their fallen technological creations like a parent as if they had lost a child.

The tide was soon being swayed in favour of the monsters from outer space and the people of Japan found their numbers alarmingly decreasing.

*

Dublin, Ireland.
They drank.
A lot.

*

Glasgow, Scotland.
Thunder and lightning ignited the skyline as the daylight evaporated and Scotland's largest city played home to a panoramic exodus.

The rain poured down hard and the only blessing it gave was that it began to wash away the blood that was being spilt from any of those brave enough to take stand against the invaders.

The Xironets used brutal force to wipe down any fighter who dare oppose them.

If Glaswegians loved one thing, however; it was there home. And she was to be defended.

Children were turned into heroes as they charged towards the beasts from every direction. Men and women raided the local pubs to use bottles and broken glass as make-shift weapons.

The Scottish were defiant.

Loyalty to their people coursed through their veins.

A small band of freedom fighters dislocated themselves from the main pack of aggressors and took the nonsensical approach to fight the alien attackers with left over marketing material from the shambolic 2016 EU Referendum.

From out of the corner of a bystander's eye, all she could see was that of a Xironet being swamped by a sea of 'Remain' propaganda material.

At least it came in useful for something, she thought.

*

Rome, Italy.

The Heaven's wept like machine gun fire over one of the most famous cities that Europe had to offer.

From atop the Pantheon, Xironets leapt to the war torn streets below, slicing and piercing the skin of the defenders of earth, the monster's minds filled with glee that this planet would soon be their own and their King's life renewed once more.

The Coliseum, once home to Gladiators and warriors of old, was now an arena of humans versus giant creatures from the farthest reaches of space.

The rain spat like acid in the face of the evil beasts as heaps of youths, who could normally be found spraying graffiti around the backstreets of the infamous walls of Rome, were now rallying together to defend those who couldn't fight. If one were to look closely enough, however, the elderly were proving to be worthy fighters as they found their spirits propel them to strike for the home they held so close to their hearts.

It was proving too much, though…the people needed a miracle.

They needed the guidance of the Lord.

Outside the steps of Vatican City, in the hallowed vision of St. Peter's Basilica, a mass of those in need fell to their knees, seeking the wisdom of their Pope.

They prayed quickly, for the Xironets were charging up behind them.

In a move that had surprised the Camerlengo and the College of Cardinals, Pope John Paul XXVI, had decided that God's will was not for Him to come and save them but for the people to save themselves.

The Pope had then subsequently announced that he was not going into hiding but was going to fight side by side with his people.

The Pope, alone in his sanctum, privately left a message with God, hoping He would return his call but quietly held his reservations

He gathered the Cardinals at the main entrance of the Vatican and anointed each of them with a holy cross to attack with.

On his count, they opened the doors, and he led his men through the gates of heaven and into the streets of hell.

*

Magaluf, Spain.

The teenagers and party lovers had desperately tried to get home to their families and loved ones. No matter how much they loved drinking, when the time came to breathe your last breath, the teens wanted nothing more than their mother's touch and father's advice.

Since all the planes had been grounded for what appeared to be indefinitely, there was no chance of any of them reaching home in time before they perished.

The youngsters had all made their phone calls home to say what could probably be their last goodbyes. The booze lovers then did the only thing their generation was most beloved for; they partied. They raided the local shops of every last drop of booze available.

Though the Xironets had invaded Spain and its neighbouring islands, the hell raisers of Magaluf had chosen not to fight. Instead, they took to their hotel rooms, filled the bathtubs with booze, cranked the volume as loud as was physically possible and began the party of a lifetime.

If they were going to die young, then they were going to do so with one last notch on their bed post and a beautiful beer buzz in their brain as they prepared to face the grim reaper.

*

Rapid City, South Dakota.

They were minutes away from storming the ground above; all they needed were a few final checks. The men had instructed the women and children to stay in the bunker and not to open the doors unless they heard the secret password uttered from one of the husbands.

189

There were enough supplies of canned goods and bottled water to keep the families going for years without having to venture out into civilisation. Littering the boxes around the floor were board games for the kids, books and movies for the adults and a small room for the comfort of the family dogs.

Everything was in place.

These were the Preppers.

And they had been preparing themselves for this day for years, even decades.

And unlike some, they were not afraid.

They were ready.

The local gun laws of the city were some of the most relaxed in the United States and this meant the preppers could use what ammunition their imaginations let them. When the television simulcast had begun, the preppers wasted no time in picking up their families and heading straight for their reinforced bunkers.

All of the men in this particular faction of preppers held blue collar jobs at the local DIY store and had often been widely mocked by their peers for their idealism of becoming a survivalist. Their wives had been quite happy for their spouses to take camping trips out into the wild, they presumed they were simply chewing the fat or enjoying a few beers or beef jerky under the stars.

In truth, it had been much more. The men honed their skills at tying knots, at seeing who could fashion a stable harness at rapid speed and which one of them could light a fire with bare essentials. Each of them had a flare for a particular skill that the others did not and together they formed a formidable team.

Over the years, while the wives sipped wine and gossiped about the local neighbours, and the kids were happily playing soccer in the yard, the men had pooled their money together to build the ultimate safe house for when the inevitable would come.

When it came to guns, however, they were all on the same page.

They stood at the bottom of the bunker, their guns and rifles ready in hand.

"Ready?"

"Ready."

They charged up the steps and opened the doors onto the world surrounding them. It was a scene of biblical proportions.

The men opened fire.

The Xironets were shot down in stunning succession.

The preppers were protecting their homes.

They were protecting their way of life.

They were protecting their families in hope of living in the new tomorrow.

And if they couldn't do that; then they would die trying.

But defeat wasn't an option.

*

Downing Street, London.

No one could believe it had come to this. The notion that the military were being overpowered was one thing but to have ordinary citizens taking to the streets to fight in arm-to-arm combat was truly something else.

Cedar Manvoid had not planned on fighting in any sense of the word. His plan was to run and run hard. He had briefly felt a pang of anguishing guilt when he had witnessed Her Majesty the Queen riding on horseback and leading her guardsman into the fray. She had wielded a beautiful sword with stunning skill as she lead them directly into the firing line, counteracting any hit that the Xironets had dealt her.

More fool her, Cedar thought.

His plan was to slip down a manhole and take refuge in the sewers of London until the whole thing had hopefully blown over. Though he had a monumental fear of rats, Cedar was more than happy to make home with them for a while rather than die.

He had even left his wife behind.

He crouched as low as he possibly could, hoping to conceal himself from the oncoming slaughterers with the pounding rain now cascading from the heavens above.

"Cedar fucking Manvoid!" he heard a voice cry out from behind him.

Barbara Fisher came into his field of vision. "What the fuck are you doing?"

"I'm running, Barbara," he blurted out. "You know it's the only thing to do." He noticed she was carrying a small hand gun in her right hand.

"Are you not fighting? Are you not playing out your swan song with great pride?"

"Like fuck am I!" Cedar cried out.

He then noticed that from where Barbara stood, soaking wet and motionless, her eyes darted from his gaze to that of something behind him. He dared to chance a look over his shoulder. What he hoped not to see, however, was absolutely what he was witnessing. Only a few dozen yards from where he was, a Xironet stood panting, salivating at its mouth.

Cedar began to weep, begging for his life. "Please, please," he wailed, arms flailing in the air. "Take her, take her, you don't want me, please, please don't kill me."

"Cedar?!" Barbara gasped, utterly stunned at the new, shameful low Cedar had sunk too.

Cedar doubted the beast could understand him but still he continued his harrowing cry for help. "Don't kill me! Don't kill me! Take her! Anything, I'll do anything you ask!"

Barbara couldn't stand it any longer. "Cedar," she barked, drawing his attention. "I hope you rot in hell you forlorn fucking piece of shit!"

She fired the gun.

The bullet landed straight in his forehead.

She felt a tinge of uneasiness at killing a man, of taking a life; she had never done it before. But she found she quite liked the feeling, especially when the man she just killed was willing to allow an alien aggressor to take hers.

She cocked her gun and took off her heels and started running at the Xironet before her.

She screamed at the beast, wildly firing at the monster's torso, bracing herself to become a ghost on these desperate streets.

*

A bead of sweat etched its way down Chilvers' forehead. He and his fellow would-be-rescuers had taken a brief refuge behind a brick wall, hoping to seek out Mark who was still hostage under the control of an injured Xironet.

"Can you see him?" Tom yelled, struggling to be heard over the sound of the fighting.

"He's over there!" Matt quipped, his faith rising only slightly in that they might just be able to bring Mark back from the near clutches of death.

Mark was visible, but only just.

As the Xironet had taken to the streets to complete its master's wish of exterminating the human race, it had come under attack from a bedraggled crew of heroic warriors.

"They must be trying to save him," Tom said.

The Xironet ripped a woman's arm from her sockets as she cried out in pain and fell back down to the ground. Mark, who was slumped in the grasp of the beast's arm, was struggling to break free of the death-like grip.

"We haven't much time," Matt feared.

*

Richard ran as fast he could through the density of the battle. He fired shots with alarming accuracy at any Xironet who came into focus. He quickly learned that the grasshopper-like gargoyles had apparently very weak skulls, so it was there that he aimed his bullets.

His mission was to rendezvous with the Wongtoks and order his strike team to assist them to the main bulkhead ship hovering miles above them.

As he raced on through the terrain, his phone buzzed.

"Yes?" Richard answered.

"Sir," came the voice. "It's the safe house. It was breached."

"What?"

"We tried to stop them. But..."

"The boys? My son? His friends?"

"They're not here, sir."

"What do you mean...they're not there?"

"They've gone. They must have escaped. There are no bodies."

"They're alive then. Find them, captain."

He shut the call off and doubled over, placing his hands on his knees to catch his breathe.

They're alive, he thought. *They're out there somewhere.*

As he gasped a few more much needed breaths of oxygen, he eyed something out in the distance through the carnage of chaos.

The Wongtoks.

*

People around the little blue beings could only marvel at what they were seeing.

The Wongtoks moved with awesome agility and decisive dexterity against their seven-foot opponents. The Xironets aggressively waved their powered staffs in the air in blind hope of trying to hit the little blue blobs but to no avail.

As the Wongtoks provided the distraction, freedom fighters launched from behind to deliver killer blows to the beasts.

For now, the Wongtoks held the upper hand but it wouldn't be long before they would become outnumbered and their adversaries would wear them down.

The Wongtoks needed to get up to the ship.

And they needed to get up there now.

*

Chilvers peered over the brick wall that they were perched behind and scanned the garden for anything that could be used as weapon. He found nothing.

Though his legs were aching, he pulled himself over the wall and looked over to the next door's garden.

Perfect.

As luck would have it, these neighbours seemed to be home. A middle-aged man with enough of a spread to conclude that he enjoyed many a can of beer was breaking apart his particularly impressive washing line and subsequently handing out the remnant metal bars to what Chilvers suspected must have been his kids.

"Tell your mother to stay inside with baby Daniel," the man shouted out.

Two lads, around aged twenty, were donning cricket helmets and protective padding as their father instructed them of what to do when they were to engage the alien invaders.

Chilvers felt his voice call out. "Excuse me, could I… um…have a few of those bars? Please? Me and my friends need a weapon."

The man stared at Chilvers, which caused him to feel quite imitated considering what was happening around them.

"Our friend," Chilvers gulped. "He's been kidnapped. We're going to go and get him back."

The middle-aged man broke out in a smile worthy of greeting an old friend.

"Come on and grab what you need," he yelled. "Boys, pass him a bar."

His sons did as they were instructed and passed some homemade weapons over to Chilvers and his newly joined friends.

"Thanks," Chilvers managed to say, preparing to head over the wall and rescue Mark.

A hand tapped him on the shoulder. "Wait there," the man shouted out to the geeks.

Chilvers saw him help his sons over the wall and quickly dart back over to the sliding patio door and where a woman stood clutching a baby. "I love you," the man told the baby. "And I love you, too," he whispered to his wife.

He then turned over to Chilvers. "You say your friend needs help?"

"Yes," Chilvers replied.

"We'll help you," he squawked, climbing over the wall, readying his weapon. "Let's go get these fuckers!"

*

The Wongtoks found themselves being backed into a corner, a part of them was desperately urging their fighting instincts to come to the surface, while another part of them was anxiously trying to protect the tiny crystal from falling into the wrong hands.

A Xironet with a grudge to bear suddenly threw two of its fellow members aside and howled at the sight of the Wongtoks.

The tiny beings instantly recognized the predator as one of the commanders from their enslavement back home on Zolandor.

This beast was clearly here with one intent only; to kill.

The Wongtoks slowly edged themselves backwards, minds racing to quickly to think how they could get themselves out of this predicament. Their little hearts shattered every time a brave soul attempted to help them from the grasps of the Xironet but whoever tried was quickly disposed of.

The beast had them exactly where it wanted them. The thirst for blood flooded the Xironets eyes, devoid of any compassion or self-awareness.

This beast was here to settle the score.

It growled with a snarl as it stretched its muscular torso to its full capacity, staggering over the Wongtoks like none ever had done so before.

Just then, four shots rang out in expeditious succession.

The Xironets head turned away from the shots but it was too late. The shots to the skull exposed its moss-coloured brain only to be fired at again by three more bullets.

The Xironet fell into a messy heap on the floor.

The Wongtoks looked up.

"Hello, there," Richard exclaimed.

*

Chilvers, Matt and Tom were more than happy for their new middle-aged comrade to lead the charge, not because their courage had dwindled but simply because he seemed to be some sort of madman as he swung his metal pole around, knocking Xironets over with supreme force.

"Is that your friend?" he yelled, pointing over to the captive Mark.

"It is," Tom replied, palm sweaty from holding the pole.

"Then let's get him!"

The man and his two sons charged at the Xironet whilst aggressively thrashing their weapons in every direction.

Some blows knocked the beast off its footing.

Others missed altogether.

As the geeks joined the fray, Tom, being the shortest of the maddening rescuers, snuck under the Xironets arm and ran a knife straight through the claw of the beast. As it screeched out in pain, the monster dropped Mark to the floor, knocking him unconscious.

With a killer blow, one of the man's sons landed a strike of the metal pole directly on the Xironets head, cracking it into two.

"Your friend okay?" the man asked.

"He should be," Matt replied, desperately trying to bring him round.

"If you have to, you can take him back to my house, my wife is there, she will help you," he reassured them.

"Thank you," Chilvers said with half a smile.

"See you on the other side," the man fired back, half smiling himself.

With that, he took his sons farther into the battlefield to no doubt save somebody else.

"That was quite something," Matt quipped.

"You'd be amazed what people will do when they need to," Tom replied.

Chilvers gently slapped Mark on the face. "MARK!" he screamed loudly, trying to think of anything to get him to come round. "WAKE UP!"

Mark's eyes shot open like he had just been pumped full of an adrenalin shot. He gasped a full breath of air and took a moment to steady himself.

"Mark, it's Tom, it's okay, everything's okay, you're safe now."

Mark, still lying on the ground, gazed upon the sky before him and pointed to what he knew the others hadn't seen yet.

Thousands more Xironet pods landing on earth.

Mark closed his eyes, a wave of exhaustion washing down upon him.

"I don't think we're going to win this," Mark uttered. "I don't think we're going to win it at all."

*

Dudley, West Midlands.

The council estate in the heart of the Black Country had seen its fair share of ups and downs. With thirty-nine underage pregnancies in the last twelve months and ninety-one percent of the residents on the dole, the estate had been on national television news with a film crew documenting the lives of the residents.

The Dope heads, Dossers and Dirty Doxies of Dudley had taken the country by storm in a media sensation. While most of the people living there had lapped up their newly found celebrity status, two of the locals had been mortified by what had happened.

Karen and Phil had lived in the block of flats since they had first married nearly forty years ago. They loved their home and they loved each other, unconditionally.

They were working class to the core and those values flowed through their veins.

Phil had been a factory worker all his life and had taken early redundancy when the firm closed down. He hadn't rested for too long though and quickly took a job as a labourer with a friend.

Karen had been a cleaner for nearly all of her fifty-eight years and though part-time, she now volunteered at the local church and community library to fill her time.

They had refused to be part of the documentary but also refused to leave their homes.

And that wasn't changing today.

They were the only residents left on the estate when the Xironet search pod landed in the middle of the car parking area below. This was their home, and like a good captain who went down with his ship, they would rather die in their living room than on some grass bank.

Karen looked through the curtains to see the alien invaders beginning their search. Though she, nor her husband, was in the best of health, they would do what they could to defend their lives. She dashed through the living room and into the hallway where she hammered on the bathroom door.

"Phil," she called out in her squeaky, cartoon-like voice and raised her volume to compensate for her husband's bad hearing.

"Phil, Phil! The aliens are coming."

No reply.

"Phil, the aliens are coming. Stop having a shit!"

"What?"

"The aliens are coming!"

"What?"

"The aliens are here to kill us!"

"Yes, I am having a shit!"

Karen covered her face as the front door to the flat burst open and three Xironets with laser guns marched in.

The beasts towered over Karen, who at a mere five-foot-two didn't seem any match for the monsters.

However, nothing could keep working class lasses down.

She wiped the blood from her face and armed herself with two kitchen knives. Karen then eyed them with pure, violent rage. This wasn't the first time Karen had been in a fight, far from it. She had seen her fair share of bar brawls over the years. "You don't scare me," she announced, altering her tone to show no fear. "Now, come here... mommy's hungry," she boomed, repeating the line she had told any drunken slob who dared to raise their fist to her in the local.

The kitchen knives flew through the air as their owner launched herself toward the horrifying giants before her.

CHAPTER FIFTEEN

A new wave of thunder erupted from the charred skyline showing no remorse in its wake of destruction. The foreboding darkness enslaved any hint of light that dared to show itself. Mother Nature had never looked so ravaged and willing to surrender.

But still; the people fought on.

And now; their numbers were begging to wane.

The unstoppable force that was the Xironet army mercilessly tore down any human rebel fighter that attempted to savage the beasts.

Earth's darkest hour was quickly approaching.

The end was nigh.

The people needed a miracle of unprecedented proportions.

At the eruption of the battlefield, the geeks summoned what failing strength they had left to try and counter any attack made by the demons before them.

It was becoming too much.

They weren't fighters.

The geeks weren't built for this sort of thing.

But still…they carried on. Willing their bodies to go on that little bit farther.

Matt suddenly dropped to his knees, exhaustion, excruciating pain and dwindling hope marooning his body.

"I'm done," he gasped, eyes burning from the pain. "I'm done, I can't carry on." Quietly, he began to sob.

Tom quickly knelt down to his aid and tried to bring Matt back to his feet. "Come on, come on! This isn't how it's supposed to end! We don't finish this way! Not us! Get back on your feet!"

"I can't, Tom," Matt sobbed. "I'm sorry but I just can't."

"It doesn't end like this," Tom boomed in his ear. "It ends differently than this! Trust me!"

Matt didn't even look up. "What are you talking about? How do you know how it's going to end? Face it, Tom, it's over. We're done for. The world is done for. Accept it."

Chilvers desperately wanted to share in Tom's hope for winning this war but he just couldn't summon his spirit to do so.

As the Xironets began to encroach ever closer, like a pack of hyenas circling their prey, Chilvers felt the last spark of faith dim out. "That's it," he murmured to himself. "This is how we go."

Chilvers knew it was close.

There was nothing that could be done.

For better or for worse, the boys were about to have their lives cut short by a ravenous pack of devils from another planet.

Death was about to become the defining verse of their saga.

Chilvers rallied his friends around him, each standing back to back in order to face the Xironets. The boys took one final battle-ready stance; much like their heroes did in the movies of old.

None of them could deny the suffocating sense of fear that coursed through their bloodstreams and each of them could only hope that the Wongtoks would be successful in their mission of eradicating the Xironets once and for all and bring peace to the planet.

Their only regret was that they wouldn't be alive to see it.

The Xironets inched closer.

"Any last words?" Chilvers threw out.

Mark closed his eyes. "Ten hail Mary's and five of our Father's."

"What is that?" Tom screamed.

"It's part of the rosary or...something like that," Mark replied.

"Are you religious?"

"No, but I am now. Just in case."

The last image that the boys would see was to be six Xironet beasts crouching themselves on their musical legs, drawing their bodies closer to the ground in order to gain more strength when leaping towards them.

The streets that they had once called home were now a picturesque inferno of a restless man's waking nightmare.

The Xironets salivated at the mouth as the anticipation of the kill grew closer, the alien evils were doing nothing more than teasing the boys, tantalizing them to the prospect of death.

And then, in unison, the Xironets pounced.

What happened next, the boys would only be able to later recall happening in slow-motion. As if it didn't really happen.

As the Xironets flew through the air, ready to sink their piercing fangs into the boys, a military truck harpooned its way through the atmosphere and sent the creatures hurtling towards the ground. The truck then reversed itself over the monsters and revved back up again to desecrate them under the weight of the machine.

As the Xironets lay twitching in a pool of their own blood, a familiar pair of shoes stepped out of the jeep, followed by eight little blue feet.

"I didn't know I had it in me," Richard proclaimed, a little shook up but still in control of his emotions.

"You don't know how happy we are to see you, Richard," Chilvers hollered.

"Hi, dad," Tom added, heart beating faster than a marathon runner.

Richard quickly surveyed all the boys for any injuries as the Wongtoks waddled over to greet their old friends in the midst of their heartbreak that was undoubtedly to follow.

"Everybody okay?" Richard asked.

"We're fine," Matt lied, knowing how their mental health was severely dwindling. "We're all okay, honestly."

Richard peered out over the war raging on. He turned back to the boys. "We've had some setbacks but we're here now. It's time to put your little friend's plan into action. It has to be now or I fear it won't happen at all."

"We're ready," the chief Wongtok announced.

Richard ushered the group to seek brief refuge behind a derelict wall of an old factory, providing them with a few minutes of respite from the devastation behind them.

"Right," Richard commanded. "This is how it's going to play out. I've got a fighter pilot en-route to these coordinates in less than five minutes. God willing, we have to try and keep alive till then. When he's here, the Wongtoks will board the jet and he will fly them up to the underbelly of that bloody ship up there and then... well...they take it from there. It's over to you from then on. Do what you have to do with that little crystal and... well...save this world." Richard offered a lop-sided smile. "Sound simple enough, huh?"

"We will complete this mission and repay our debt to you," Harry Wongtok concluded.

"We would have used our own ship," Gary Wongtok added meekly. "But it is...as you say...out of commission."

Richard pulled up his sleeve and clocked the seconds on his watch, a countdown timer he had set a few minutes ago. "If we're going to do this," he echoed. "Then it has to be now. I'm sorry." He glanced at his digital watch once more. "My pilot will be here in... exactly three minutes and thirty-six seconds..." He eyes grew remorseful. "I'm sorry, boys, but...I'll give you...a few minutes to say your goodbyes. This is how it has to be. I'll be just over here."

As Richard paced away, taking a call on his phone and watching out for any encroaching Xironets, the boys found themselves alone with their tiny friends.

They were alone with them for the final time.

Boy looked at alien.

Alien looked at boy.

Silence hung in the air.

"I, um," Chilvers began, not knowing where the next words would come from and sensing a lump form in his throat. "I guess this is the last time we will see each other."

Bruce Wongtok nodded, slowly, and only once, his eyes full of sorrow. "It is, indeed, my friend."

Matt closed his eyes, blocking out the screams and gun shots ringing out from only a few dozen metres behind them. "I...we...we don't want you to go. We want you to stay... stay here...with us."

The Wongtoks smiled, all at once. A smile that was warm and comforting. It was a smile that might have suggested to an old friend that everything was going to be okay. It was a smile that might have reassured a bird with a broken wing that it was okay to fly again. It was a smile that felt like the reciprocated love of a parent to a child in the face of overwhelming grief, a grief that no child should face at such a tender age. It was smile that said... *please...don't worry...don't worry yourself so much.*

Mark's lips trembled with emotion, emotion that he could not control. "I…we…um…I'll miss you. We will miss you."

"And we, you," the Wongtoks concurred.

From out of their peripheral vision, the boys could see that Richard was making his way back to them.

The end beckoned.

The boys didn't like it.

Though their hearts broke into a million pieces at the prospect of saying goodbye, the boys knew, deep down, that no matter how hard one tried to resist the flow of time, or resist the pull of the future tide, there a came a point in every person's life when you simply had to let go.

One had to realise that life would never be the same.

Realise, that eventually, it might be okay. Time might make it okay.

Realise that…in the end…nothing lasts forever and that though hearts got shattered and rebuilt over the course of a lifetime, in the end, no one ever really got it right.

They could only try their hardest.

They could only give it their all.

But still…it didn't help how they felt now.

A sense of loss that they felt could never be replaced.

They fought the final few moments.

They felt the door to boyhood innocence close for the final time.

It felt so definite. It felt like such a burden to bear.

But now…it was time to say goodbye.

It was time to grow up.

It was time to let go.

And not look back.

The boys knew that they could never look back.

Never.

"It's time," they heard Richard say.

207

Chilvers embraced each of the Wongtoks in a hug, a hug like no other, a hug of true, unquestioned friendship.

"Thank you," he whispered to them.

Behind him, Matt and Mark followed suit, saying farewell to the creatures of which they felt an unbreakable, earth shattering bond.

Not everyone did the same, however. Off to the side, an unsettling silence surrounded Tom that disturbed the rest of the boys.

Chilvers realised that Tom hadn't uttered a single word. Not one.

"Tom," he questioned carefully. "Aren't you going to say anything? Aren't you going to say goodbye? It's the least you can do. They're going to sacrifice themselves to save us. Say something."

"No."

"No?! What do you mean…no?"

"I won't say goodbye," Tom murmured. "Because… I'm going to be the one to do it."

Chilvers felt his jaw go slack. "You're going to do fucking what?"

Tom held his ground. "I'm going to go up there. Trust me." He turned to the Wongtoks. "I'm doing this. Please, give me The Aithēr."

Before the Wongtoks could speak, Richard placed a calming hand on his son's shoulder and gently squeezed it, a squeeze of reassurance. "Son, I know that you've been through a lot, we all have, but it doesn't mean that you can go around saying stuff like that. It's not funny. It's upsetting."

"Dad," Tom mumbled. "I don't expect you to understand but…"

"But what?" Richard snapped. "But what, son?"

"But, this is something that I need to do. All I can remember you saying from when I was a kid was one thing…you said 'sometimes, you've simply got to do, what you've got to do…' And this is one of those times in life when I've got to do just that. This is something I've got to do. I can't put it any other way."

Everyone simply stood stunned. Confused at what was now playing out before their eyes.

Matt shook his head violently and buried his eyes deep into his hands, desperately trying to rid himself of the absurdity of the situation he now found himself in. "Tom," he screamed. "Can you hear yourself? Do you even know what you're saying?"

Mark rubbed his temple, a headache beginning to form, more from annoyance than anything else. "Tom, don't be a prick," he urged. "Are you trying to get some attention or something? Cause if you are, this is not the time to do it. Are you trying to be selfish? Cause if you are, then you're doing a splendid job."

"No," Tom shot back. "It's not that! It's not any of those things! It couldn't be farther from it. I don't think any of you would understand, you could try, but none of you would."

"Then make us understand," Chilvers calmly offered.

Tom opened his mouth, waiting for the words to arrive. His inner most demons betrayed him, however, as nothing came. Even though he was surrounded by his best friends and his father, he was still reluctant to bare his soul whole, for fear of what he might find.

But still, he prevailed.

"I need to do this," he began, eyes meandering all over the place, not wanting to look at anyone. "I believe that my life has been building up to this moment, it's been leading up to it since the day I was born. This very choice

I'm about to make is one that will define me; it will make me who I am…who I want to be. It will make me whole. My entire life, all I've been doing is coasting my way through…ambling along from one day to the next, not really knowing who I am or where I'm going."

Richard couldn't help but interject; he had enough of his son's delusions of grandeur. "THAT'S WHAT LIFE IS, SON! YOU WAKE UP, YOU GO TO WORK, YOU GO HOME AND THE NEXT DAY, YOU DO IT ALL OVER AGAIN…IF YOU'RE LUCKY!"

"Not everyone," Tom pleaded. "I believe that some people are built for better things. They have an awakening inside of them, calling them on for something more, something that other people can't possibly define."

Matt's cheeks flushed with superstition. "And you think you're one of those people?!"

"Not necessarily," Tom quipped with a shrug of the shoulders. "But I do know that I'm not one who longs for mediocrity and I am certainly not going to settle for it. I have a chance to make it all right, to make it all better and when a chance like that comes along…only a fool lets it pass by."

"ARE YOU HAVING A FUCKING EXISTENTIAL CRISIS?" Mark screeched at the top of his lungs, tiring of this talk. "Because if you are, then get some help. We'll get you some help. We'll help you sort out a therapist or something."

"Your friend's right," Richard stated, trying to bring some calm to the situation and hoping to remind his son of a halcyon time. "You've suffered a trauma and-"

"Stop telling me how to feel," Tom requested, a little more exasperation in his words than he had intended. "I'm taking that crystal and I'm going to see this thing through. Why won't any of you listen to me?"

"And then what?" Chilvers roared, his patience being tested with every syllable that left Tom's mouth. "You live on forever as a martyr?"

"No...no, no, no. I will become something much more than a title or a pre-fix before my name."

"BUT YOU ARE GOING TO FUCKING DIE!" Matt boomed.

"I know but I've made up my mind on this since late last night. Before we all fell asleep. My death will have meaning and then my life will have meaning."

"But why Tom? Just tell us! Why?"

Richard grabbed his son by the scruff of his neck, signalling for the madness to cease. "This stops now! Right now! The Wongtoks will complete their mission, they WILL SEE THIS THING THROUGH...NOT YOU! NOT YOU! Listen to me, son, you've got everything to live for."

"Not everything," Tom scolded. "All my life all I ever wanted to do was what any child wants to accomplish in life...to make their parents proud of them. You grow up, you try and become a good person, and you try and do the right thing and help others and most importantly, make your parents proud.

"What else is there? Really? But...what if...what if you can't do those things? What if I will never be able to make you proud of me or worse...what if I will never be able to make myself happy? I am a young boy who should be on his trajectory of feeling like I am going to live forever but instead I am already marred by my disappointments.

"This is my chance to do something right for once and make it last forever. I can save the world, dad, and... well...more importantly...the world can save me."

No one took their eyes off Tom. Only Chilvers tried to articulate something into anything. "So, you…um… what I…you…"

Tom, now the epitome of a young boy crossing the threshold onto the void of manhood, silently reached for the satchel on his back. He held onto it for a moment, a moment that seemed to last a lifetime, he then gripped it firmly and passed it to Chilvers.

"There's one more thing," he stated. "I need you to promise me that you will make this happen."

"Make what happen?" Chilvers quizzed.

"Just look."

Chilvers opened the satchel and fingered through the documents that lay inside.

"What…what are these?"

"Blueprints," Tom confessed. "Blueprints for my final wish."

"And what's that?"

Tom took a deep breath, exhaling slowly. "I…well," he stuttered before clearing his throat. "I want to be made into an action figure."

"YOU WANT TO BE MADE INTO A FUCKING WHAT?" Richard balled.

Once again, Tom didn't back down, determined to stick to his guns. "I want to be made into an action figure. I want my own toy line. I'm not a movie star or a superhero, so, this I suppose, is my only chance. I want it to be grand. I want it to be magic. I can live forever. I can live forever in the imaginations of children. It's the closest thing to immortality I think I'll ever know."

"BUT YOU WILL BE FUCKING DEAD!" Now it was Chilvers' turn to chime in his anger.

Tom simply shrugged his shoulders. "I know…I know." He then inhaled a deep gasp of air. "All the details are in there, and a letter too, but don't read that until after."

While no one could truly grasp what was truly transpiring before them; a war ravaging their home world, a friend confessing of his innate desire to commit self-sacrifice, no one had noticed one, minor detail that carried a fair amount of significance.

The Wongtoks were gone.

When the minute aliens had heard of their new found friends intentions to fulfil his heart's destiny, they had quietly scuttled away and made their way to the fighter jet that Tom's father had spoken of.

It looked like they might just make it, too.

They ran as fast as their tiny padded feet would carry them. They darted through the mass of bloodied destruction and leapt up onto the jet.

That was all the pilot had needed to fire up. Richard had previously told him that four, benevolent creatures would need a lift up to the ship that hovered in the skyline. When the pilot saw some strange beings jump up on his jet, he wasted no time in getting off the ground as fast as he could.

He was under strict instructions not to return to the ground for any reason, once he was up, his only destination was the underbelly of the ship that so threatened them all.

As the jet fully lifted off the ground, the pilot felt the tail of his jet duck down slightly. The pilot presumed it was the funny looking little aliens shifting their weight, but in truth, it was something far more daunting.

From the back of the fighter craft, where the Wongtoks were clinging to the bulk of the jet, the aliens felt their hearts plunge at the sight of Tom attaching himself to the rear head with a self-made harness fashioned out of rope.

If anything, Tom only looked remorseful as he hung on tightly to a wing with one hand and reached for The Aithēr crystal with the other. For fear of falling, the Wongtoks couldn't take the tiny crystal back in their grasp and they could only wince at what they knew in their hearts was coming.

"I'm sorry," Tom cried, never before meaning the words like he did now. "I am so sorry."

Tom shut his eyes and swung out as far as he could, knocking the Wongtoks off balance and sending them flying back down towards the ground. They fell a few hundred metres and landed on the ground with a definitive thud.

Chilvers and rest of the group raced through the chaos to find the Wongtoks. They were mostly unhurt, just in pain from the fall.

"What happened?" Richard screamed. "What just happened?"

"He's up there," the chief Wongtok sighed. "He's up there and he's got The Aithēr."

"He just left," Matt stammered. "He saw that you weren't here and just left. He didn't say anything."

Mark yanked on Richard's jacket, vying for his attention. "Call your pilot! Tell him to stop! Tell him to fucking stop."

"I can't," Richard wavered. "He's already up there."

Chilvers, Matt, Mark, and the Wongtoks could only stare up at their friend.

Richard simply could not believe his eyes.

As Tom reached the aperture of the Xironet ship, he knew that there really was no going back at this point.

From here on out, it was only the brave allowed.

Tom felt that time was slowing down; his internal body clock perhaps aware that his final few minutes were upon him and his final chime would ring out.

He almost didn't realise that the fighter jet had left him and he was now clutching the inner skeleton of what would be his final ascent. Without being consciously aware it, Tom began to climb.

As his eyes were drawn to the encroaching darkness looming above him, he felt an overwhelming sense of sadness pull down on his heart. He longed to look back but he knew that he couldn't. He longed to gaze upon the faces of his friends and his father one last time but he knew it would never be.

For them, he pondered, life was about to do what it did best…it was going to take something away. Life had a habit of doing that. It gave you things for a while but then as one grew older, eventually everything around them faded to dust.

For Tom, he couldn't have felt more prepared.

He felt a slight twinge of pain in his fist from where he was gripping The Aithēr too tightly. He wondered what a fleeting moment of empowerment would feel like when he used the crystal to its full vantage.

He would soon find out.

An idea dropped into his head that this was the first time that he had ever really contemplated death in any philosophical fashion. He had experienced the pain of losing people for sure…

Memories surged through his mind of loved ones long gone.

He wondered where they were.

He wondered where he was going.

Tom had only thought about death once before and it wasn't in the most of conventional circumstances.

He had arrived home from school one evening to find that his Aunty was visiting his mother. Closer inspection found that his mother had allowed his much younger cousins to play with some of his collectables and merchandise. As most youngsters are prone to not having a concept of caring for their toys, Tom's cherished collectables lay in tatters on the kitchen table.

For Tom, someone who was defined by his collection of memorabilia, he had been utterly crushed. He tried, in vein, to glue them all back together but in the end it had been a thankless task.

For some, they were defined by their talents on the football pitch, for some it was their job or chosen career path, for others it was their spouse or partner. For Tom, it was his toys. It always would be and there was nothing that would ever change that.

They were a way for him to escape from the pain and melancholy of the real world.

His passion for collecting was his way of running away from the truth.

His collecting was him. And he had loved every minute of it.

Tom had longed since known that his passions had made him a nerd. A geek. An outcast. But Tom had always stridden to find his own voice. To seek out his individuality.

As Tom continued to climb the final steps and make his way toward the King of the Xironets, he found his mind begin to trespass to places that only the most haunted of men had ever dared to tread.

He thought about the end.

Tom wondered how many people had ever died how they really wanted to. He thought about how many people had agonized over their final minutes, of whether they fretted the prospect of death or whether they faced it with dignity. He then thought that perhaps it was personal to that soul alone and perhaps other people shouldn't intrude so much.

In films and television, death was often so overdramatized. Usually an actor was mugging the shot in hope of reaping some awards or good reviews when their work came out. He thought it would probably be nothing like the movies. Nothing ever was. There were very few happy endings in the world. Tom knew that there were only small recesses of joy that made up the big picture. He knew that now and he knew it so young.

Tom found himself wondering about Heaven and whether it really did exist. Strangely, he mused, he found that he wasn't particularly worried about whether it was real or not. He hoped that he would leave his fingerprints on the lives of others for a while.

Tom realised what the cruel mistress of life really was; it wasn't the fact that life took things from us…it was the fact that it forced life to go on. That it would never stop or one would never be able to reclaim the lost beauty of joy long gone.

As Tom reached the cleft of the flooring of the Xironet ship, he slowly peered over the top and eyed the surroundings. His eyes drifted and then settled on The King.

He'd found him.

It was time.

Tom lowered himself down the hatch just for a moment, enough to gather his breath and close his eyes.

When he opened them, he found that his life's passion tapped him on the shoulder one final time. He eyed the ship in all its detail. He pictured it in his hands. He pictured it with firing parts and moveable pieces. He pictured it in a stunning collector's presentation box.

Tom smiled.

"You," he whispered in the faintest of volumes. "You would make an awesome toy."

Tom raised his fist and charged towards the King.

In his fist, he ignited The Aithēr.

He let his mind go.

He let whatever was going to happen next, happen.

And then…

In that moment, Tom sacrificed himself for the greater good.

And then…

In that moment…

He became nothing.

And he became everything.

CHAPTER SIXTEEN

The silence was deafening.

Though men and women continued to battle the monsters with every drop of strength left in the marrow of their bones, Chilvers and his friends could only stare up at the ship above them.

Four agonizing minutes had passed since they had lost sight of Tom, an image that, no matter what the outcome, would be etched in their minds forever. In his heart of hearts, Chilvers knew that the last picture of their friend would be of him climbing upward toward certain doom.

They could only wonder if he would succeed in his quest or if the world would fall to her knees in stunning form.

Richard's ashen face only grew more tortured and harrowed with each passing moment. Chilvers knew that though they stood to lose a friend, it was nothing compared to the incalculable notion of losing a child. None of them could look at Richard; the geeks could barely bring themselves to look at each other.

Chilvers looked at the ship.

Still nothing.

No movement, no noise, no nothing.

He couldn't help but think that Tom might fail. That his death would be in vein.

And then...

The heavens above erupted in tyrannical fashion as the skies then waged a war with themselves. As a whirlpool of sound waves discharged from the Xironet ship, the battle being fought on ground temporarily hinted towards a lull.

From the now convulsing ship, a small, celestial light was visible through the burning sky. Seconds later, like a dying star shooting through the night, the small beacon of hovering light imploded upon itself and began to evaporate into billions of atoms through the atmosphere.

The tiny particles then absorbed back as one, holding slightly, until it finally denoted into a multitude of light. As the light hit the Xironet ship, every fragment of its structure began to crumble into a thousand pieces. An eruption of electric energy took hold of the ship until it finally gave way to a singular explosion from the epicentre.

It was happening.

Tom must have done it.

As the ship blew off into every direction, the small, vivid spectrum of light remained stagnant, refusing to move an inch.

As the ship's shrapnel began to descend towards earth, people took cover under anything they could.

Chilvers quickly lunged himself over Mark, narrowly missing a chunk of wreckage aiming for his head. Richard instinctively grabbed Matt from the falling debris and covered him with his own body, taking the brunt of anything that might hurl towards them.

As the streets caught fire once more, the Xironets were lost as to what to do. Their King and Queen were most definitely dead. The firestorm around them caught ablaze once again, and they were standing directly in the middle of it.

Chilvers dared to peer out from behind his hands that were covering his eyes, when he did; he was forced to look away.

Beside him, Matt's finger slowly rose and pointed to the tarnished horizon.

In the skyline above them, the hovering luminescence radiated a shattering manifestation of unalloyed white light.

As dust slowly evaporated, everyone around them could clearly see the Xironets lowering their weapons and swaying unsteadily on their feet. Suddenly, they stood motionless, utterly unable to move. The beasts raised their clawed hands before them and stared at the withering digits now moribund in front of them.

Around the landscape, the lightening energy that could have only come from The Aithēr cascaded toward them. The Xironets howled out in agony as the light riddled their bodies, searing through them like electricity.

As the light engulfed each of the beasts, there was a moment of suspension before finally; the beasts began to crumble to ash. The Xironets physical matter were now falling to the same fate as their master; death.

Chilvers squinted his eyes as much as he could whilst still retaining a slither of vision. As his sight fell onto the Wongtoks, he found that he was forced to look away.

As the Xironets were disintegrating to the ground, the four blue beings titled their heads up and bathed in the new light.

When the bewildering energy encased the Wongtoks, their arms jolted against themselves, as if it were too much to bear. The Wongtoks recoiled as the light tortured every cell of their body.

What happened next would become the stuff of legend.

From every component of the Wongtoks, The Aithēr's verve reverberated through them and propagated into the yonder. As the final Xironets began to disintegrate, every crack and crevice that the light touched began to shine anew.

*

Around the world the light transcended into every ruptured city, every broken street and every shattered soul that lay in wait. As the energy seeped into the soil of everything, it beckoned for the light to break free and overshadow the dominance of the darkness.

The world was beginning to be born again.

Cheers and celebrations began to fill the air as the people realised what was happening; the battle was won.

But it wasn't without cost.

Though the mystic energy paved the way for new life to blossom, it did not bring those back who had already fallen fatal to the blows dealt by the Xironets.

The victory would prove to be bittersweet.

The healing would take time.

*

Above them, the defeatist clouds began to disperse and the wretched rain started to retreat, making way for the new dawn of sunlight to break through and soak the land.

Chilvers, Matt and Mark regained themselves to their feet to witness the Wongtoks now radiating like never before. As the final droplet of light left them, they were left standing illuminated with colours that defied the mortal realm.

The Wongtoks turned to face their friends.

The boys looked at the Wongtoks.

The Wongtoks looked back, now seeing sagacious life travellers who had seen too much.

Now, the Wongtoks were looking at heroes.

Now, the Wongtoks were looking at young men. Young men, who were still standing despite facing unspeakable cataclysm and personal epic tragedy.

All eyes fixated on Richard, a man whose heart wept of unspeakable loss.

"I'm glad you boys are okay," he mustered, barely audible but with genuine sincerity. He then turned to the Wongtoks. "I'm glad you're okay, too."

The Wongtoks didn't speak. They simply nodded.

Richard couldn't bring to himself to look at the boys at the moment. Anger, sadness, frustration and every other conceivable emotion weighed down on his shoulders. He kept it together, never letting his guard down. "I have matters to sort," Richard said. "I'll arrange for any medical attention you boys need as soon as possible. No doubt this is the calm before the storm. The world will be stunned for a while but then will come the hard work. I suggest you boys take it all in. Don't be afraid to be upset. It's okay not to be okay."

The boys nodded. Each of them went to say something to Richard but he stopped them.

"Please," he whispered softly. "I know, I know." He lowered his head to the floor and when he tilted it up again he was smiling, probably because it was the only thing that was keeping him together through all this. No doubt his grief would flood him at home, suffocating him, refusing to ease up. "I suggest you boys get home to your families. Anything you need, call me."

Richard nodded to the boys and then to the Wongtoks. As he walked away he suddenly stopped. "What will I tell my wife?"

The boys didn't say anything.

"If you boys think of anything, let me know."

He looked exasperated as he turned his back and headed off to engage with his fellow officers.

Chilvers rubbed his forehead and then the thought dropped into his head. "Richard!" he called out. "Richard!"

Richard turned back around. Chilvers couldn't help but notice that the turn was a little hesitant.

As Richard made his way back to the boys and aliens, Chilvers rummaged through the satchel that Tom had given him.

"The right words," Chilvers uttered. "The right words for your wife. I think I have the right words." He produced a letter. "Well, they aren't my words. They're your son's. They're Tom's words."

Chilvers went to hand Richard the note but Richard shook his head and gestured for Chilvers to read it out loud.

Chilvers shook his head, he too sensing that he wouldn't be able to make it through reading the letter without his voice breaking or tears streaming. He had read a poem at his grandfather's funeral and it had almost killed him.

He glanced at Matt but he also waved his hands to pass on the request. And so, it fell to Mark. He took the letter and cleared his throat before readjusting his glasses on the brim of his nose.

"I'll just read it as it's written," he announced. He steadied his voice and took a breath.

The group took a moment, gathering themselves to hear the final words of their now lost friend. Even the Wongtoks carried a solemn look in their tiny eyes.

Mark began.

'Dear All,

If you're reading this letter then I can only presume that I have fulfilled my quest and hopefully destroyed the invaders to earth. Even now, that seems such a strange sentence to write.

As I write this note, I can't help but keep thinking one thing; damn, I wish I had lost my virginity. I really do. (For the love of all things sacred, make sure you three lose yours) I can only hope that there are some beauties in Heaven that will sleep with me (at least, I assume that's where I'm going but like most things in my life, I could be wrong)

To my parents, I say this; I have never felt so loved than I was when I was home. I was so proud to call you my parents and I hope you know that I will love you, always. Make sure you both take that holiday to the Caribbean you have been talking about, sell some stories to the press about me or something, really whore me out if you have too.

To my sister, I say this; when you get knocked up and have a kid, make sure it's a boy and please call it after me. It's not much to ask of you and I know that if the little squirt is called Tom, then he will no doubt grow up to be a very charming and incredibly witty guy.

When I was in the company of you, my family, I always felt like I belonged. I always felt home and that is something that I never took for granted.

Now, onto the action figure business...

When all of you get past the absurdity of the idea, I know that you will all come around to my way of thinking... but I am warning you! I don't want any of you stealing my thunder and having your own little action figures made because I will return to haunt you and make your lives a nightmare. I have stipulated very clearly in my blueprints that I want the action figure to have at least seven point of articulation and to come complete with weapons and accessories.

I suspect that you might have to gather some media promotions to get the ball rolling on the whole toy thing but hopefully the public will get behind it and then rush out to buy a little plastic version of me.

Now, I really want you to go to town on the whole merchandise thing. I MEAN IT!!! If possible, I want a whole range of toys, games, t-shirts, playing cards, mugs, and anything else that you can think of that my face could go on.

AND REMEMBER – NO ONE ELSE IS TO HAVE THEIR OWN TOY!!! AFTER ALL…DID THE REST OF YOU SAVE THE WORLD…NO…(please know I mean this with a little dash of humour but I am actually being very, very serious)

To the three of you, Chilvers, Matt and Mark, I don't really know how to say goodbye. I guess I thought that we'd all live forever and we wouldn't have to say goodbye. (Wouldn't that be a nice world to live in…where goodbyes don't exist?)

I sit here writing this note in the basement while the three of you are asleep and our alien friends are upstairs…how marvellous does that sound?!

I always knew that the three of us would have the adventure of a lifetime one day…I hope the three of you have many, many more.

I guess I would like to say that I hope you keep me in your hearts for a while but go live a life worth living, hit the highway and roll with it. (If you all would like to get a giant tattoo of my face on your chests then that is something that I wouldn't protest)

I sit here wondering if I should leave you all with some advice…I can only think of this…NEVER TRUST A MAN WHO HAS NEVER GOTTEN UP EARLY FOR WORK. (If that catches on then please trademark in my name. Many thanks)

I know that we will see each other again but I hope it isn't for a really, really long time.

Don't forget that it's always about the merch and God help you if you don't sort this action figure thing out...after all...it is the reason I have decided to sacrifice myself.

For now, over and out, Tom

P.S – If Hollywood decides to make a film about my life then that would be swell. Don't fight them. I want it to be the biggest blockbuster the world has ever seen. I do, however, have only one request...there is to be a scene in the film where I am depicted as on old man and there is only one actor I want to play me;

HARRISON FORD.

MAKE IT HAPPEN, BITCHES!

P.P.S – I love you. All of you.

Amongst the defeated wreckage on the streets, the boys and Richard found tears streaming down their cheeks, tears of pain and of joy. None of them could supress the laughter that burst from the well of their souls.

"That bastard," Mark cried out through his misty eyes, his laugh echoing all around them.

All of them could hear Tom's voice now. His passionate ways and boundless energy now playing in their minds.

"We only knew him for one day," the leader of the Wongtoks declared. "But I know that we will feel him for a lifetime."

The group's smiles soon faded as it dawned on them that they were unclear about their future with the tiny creatures.

Chilvers quickly turned to Richard. "What will happen to them?"

"I'm...I'm," Richard sighed, not wanting to complete the answer. "I'm afraid it will all be very formal no doubt. As the days pass and the world surveys the damage, the government, or what's left of it, will have all manners of tests and questions to conduct. Not only for your friends here but for you boys, too."

That didn't sit well with the geeks. Not one bit.

"So, they'll be treated like lab rats in an experiment?" Mark barked.

"But…but they're not here to kill us! They have helped us," Matt quickly protested.

"I'm afraid some people will not see it that way," Richard replied.

"He is right," Gary Wongtok said softy. "We brought this to your world. You have paid a heavy price for our presence."

"Come to think of it," Richard brooded, his eyes staying fixed on the floor. "I hate to say it…but there might be a witch hunt for you."

"What? No!"

"It's true. People will be angry at what they will have lost and will want someone or something to blame. I can hide the truth as much as possible but in the end it will be inevitable."

Raw silence followed.

Then Richard rubbed his chin. "We can't let that happen can we?"

The boys looked at him, unsure what direction he was going to take.

"If I were to 'happen' to lose sight of the little aliens and not know where they went, then there's not much I could do about it is there?"

Chilvers cocked his head. "What are you saying?"

Richard smirked, it was faint but it was there. "They need to run. They need to vanish."

"But…"

"Boys," Richard stated. "I'm afraid there is no other way."

"Their ship," Matt interjected. "Their ship isn't flyable. Where are they going to go?"

"Anywhere but here," Richard concluded. "There is no outcome that I can see ending how you want it to if they stay. I'm sorry. I'll give you a few moments."

"You're friend's father is being very kind," one of the Wongtoks stated. "I think it would be wise of us to heed to his advice."

Chilvers felt that his shoulders were once again burdened. "So, once again we face ourselves saying goodbye."

"I'm afraid so," the beings replied.

Mark felt his eyes go damp once more. He would be glad when this day was over. "Saying goodbye just seems so final."

"Then let us not say goodbye. We will see you boys again, I know it," the chief Wongtok said. "There are no words that can express our gratitude towards to you. And for Tom, he will never truly be gone. His is everywhere and in each of us. Living forever."

Richard noticed officials from every sector slowly begin to swamp the area. "It's time for you to disappear," he noted to the Wongtoks.

They nodded.

Chilvers felt himself once again lost for words as he exchanged looks with Matt and Mark. "Well, here we go again."

The Wongtoks took the hands of each of the boys and gently clasped them together. "You boys are just at the beginning."

And as quickly as they had entered their lives, the tiny blue beings from outer space now fled into the crowd and into hiding.

Their destination? The boys did not know.

It was probably best to be left that way. But somehow they knew that the tiny creatures would be okay. Deep down, they couldn't help but think that they would most definitely see them again. After all, fate had a funny habit of working things out.

The Wongtoks dashed through the crowd until eventually they disappeared forever.

"God speed," Chilvers whispered.

"I second that," Richard admitted. "You know what's funny? I could see those little aliens being made up as stuffed toys. I'm sure Tom would have collected them all." He chuckled to himself and noticed that he was being called over by an officer.

"That's my cue to leave," he confirmed. "You boys stay safe. I'll catch up with you in a little while." He patted each of them on the back and headed off to re-join his clan.

The boys were left to themselves.

Just the three of them.

It felt weird.

A silence hung in the air. Each of them glancing at one another and then to the scene around them.

"What do we do now?" Chilvers asked.

"I don't know," Matt observed.

"We could go for a beer?" Mark offered.

"But we aren't old enough to drink…" Chilvers noted.

Mark chuckled to himself. "Chilvers…I don't think anyone is going to care."

EPILOGUE

SUNRISE THROUGH THE CRACKED WINDOW AND THE DAWNING OF THE EVERYMAN WHO DESERVES HIS CALLING HORIZON

SIX MONTHS LATER...

At a supermarket in the heart of a bustling city centre, a young mother began her usual Friday morning expenditure. She had already completed the task of coffee with her mother-in-law, a laborious weekly meeting of which she was obligated to attend and then she had been to the post office, the bank and finally she found herself in the grocery isle.

She ticked items off her list but sped up her pace when she realised she was running behind to pick her youngest daughter up from the day centre. She had a few more items than normal to get today; a birthday cake, wrapping paper and birthday gifts for her son.

She couldn't believe he was already turning eight years old this year but time to contemplate that would be later with a glass of wine. Now, she had to get the toys on his birthday list he wanted so badly and for once; it would be easy.

When she reached the toy isle, she couldn't help but notice the genuine smile that broadened on her face when she started to eye the toys. Much to her satisfaction, she noted that everyone down the heaving toy section was broadly grinning. Even the most cold hearted of people let the ice melt when they saw this particular brand of toys.

The young mother picked up what she needed and headed to the check out. The cashier girl beamed like she did every time she scanned one of these toys.

The *TOM ACTION FIGURE LINE* was in full swing and available at every shop not only in the United Kingdom but worldwide. *Chilvers had kept his word.*

The *Tom Action figures* came complete with accessories and one-hundred percent likeness of the world-saving hero with whom they were based. Parents everywhere were buying the t-shirts, mugs, posters, trainers, sports goods, masks.

Like the dream he had always wanted, Tom was living on in the minds of children (and grown-up children) everywhere.

The cashier picked up the final item in the trolley, a sky blue t-shirt with Tom's face in the centre and beneath it two words imprinted that simply read; "*GEEK GOD*".

The cashier loved it.

She might just pick one up for herself.

*

In a school hall that was infamous for dire productions, a raucous audience were admitting one fact; the drama department had balls. The once farcical and uptight drama heads now lavished the shows with tongue-in-cheek humour and everyone agreed that it was actually pretty funny.

The aspiring actors were now staging 'A Midsummer Night's Dream' which, in this version, was set in Hackney with a sci-fi twist.

The school hall sat in fits of laughter as the performers didn't take it all too seriously and hammed it up at any chance they got. Everyone seemed to carry a decent sense of humour these days. It was nice. It was warming.

As the actors mugged the audience for all they were worth, they all noted how the pupils were adorned in t-shirts, badges, scarfs and bags of a former pupil who had gone down in a blaze of glory.

In earnest, it wasn't much. All they were doing was spending a few quid of their allowances on merchandise but it was enough.

Life went on. It had to.

But the fact remained that the hero had truly come home.

As the cast took their bows, the audience rose to their feet.

It was a glorious standing ovation worthy of the greats.

*

In a deserted flat in an abandoned estate, the walls lay dripping in blood.

The carpet was soaked and a distinct smell of death was pungent in the air. The alien beasts had certainly made a mess of her home but Karen wasn't going to let that small consequence factor in and force her out of her own home.

Her husband Phil had tragically passed away whilst on the loo when the beasts had attacked all those months ago. The council estate was now Karen's to rule, for no one had returned.

Karen enjoyed the quiet because she still liked her own company. Her days were spent cooking, reading and then finished off with some late night T.V.

It was around midnight when she always felt funny. Her neck would writher in pain and her eyes would become blurry. Before she drifted off to sleep, her hands would shake violently and her stomach would heave like she had never known before.

Whenever she woke up the next day, she could never recall why she ended up outside. She often wondered if the grief of losing her husband had sent her mad. Still, she wasn't going to the doctors to find out. She would carry on like she always did.

So she settled down once more for a night of unsettled sleep and she soon drifted off. It was while she was asleep that Karen unknowingly took her true form…that of a seven-foot beast with a distinct likeness to a giant grasshopper and an unquenchable thirst for little blue beings.

*

In a home that had once housed so many stories; a lingering feeling of emptiness now encompassed its only resident.

Had it been his fourth or fifth scotch? Richard didn't know and to be quite frank, he no longer cared. He sat alone like he always did in the middle of the night and hugged a bottle of cheap whiskey. His face had become craggy, tired and his eyes were now full of a bitter, distant regret.

His wife had not been able to handle the loss of a child, so she had been temporarily taken to a psychiatric ward for some more specialised care. He had sent her there with a mountain of merchandise that had been modelled after their son. He knew she would get better and return home one day but in the meantime he would continue to have an affair with whiskey on a nightly basis.

Their daughter, devastated by the loss of her younger brother, had moved out with her new husband, leaving even more of a void in their lives.

Richard chugged the glass and poured himself another. For every second of every day, he played the events over in his mind; the good, the bad and the truly horrific were always cascading through his ever restless and exhausted mind.

Why had he done it? Did he suffer? Perhaps there was a way the aliens could bring him back? What was his obsession with toys and being a hero?

So many questions...

Richard sipped from his glass and rubbed his cheek. One thing he did know was that his son had acted with compassion, kindness and selflessness on a grand scale. He knew, like the rest of the population, that these factors had been sorely missing from the world for a long time and Tom had brought them back...or perhaps he had simply reminded the world of what it was capable of?

He checked the clock on the wall. Nearly three A.M. He hadn't slept through the night in six months and doubted he ever would again. The drink helped him grab a few hours but it also settled the disturbing dreams he had been having of late.

At first they had been nightmares interjected with horrific visions. Slowly, though, the nightmares had turned to dreams. Those dreams had formed pictures and over time the pictures had formed a series of words. Now he saw those same words every night in his sleep.

He wasn't sure if they were haunting him or trying to save him. He didn't know whether they were a blessing or a curse but he slowly found himself finding comfort in the words he now saw so vividly at night.

Words that he knew were being spoken to him somehow by his son, wherever his son may be.

Richard closed his eyes and allowed himself to drift off, awaiting the arrival of that brief, inner contentment.

If somebody around the world should lose their way and fall, then anybody could find a hero deep down within themselves and rise up to answer the call.

The bottle of whiskey slipped out of Richard's hand and rolled over onto the floor. In his other hand, though deep in sleep, Richard clutched an action figure so tightly that it was almost like he was hugging his son once more.

*

On a faraway planet, millions of light-years away, four little aliens were hard at work trudging through their newly founded agricultural development regime.

The four blue beings had watched from the shadows as a doctrine of peaceful sustainability had been drawn up on planet earth. Once they were satisfied that life would continue, the blue beings had salvaged their ship in a secret hideout and gotten her ready for take-off.

They had searched as far as the stars could carry them to find a new settlement in hope of rebuilding a life. And while the beings were optimistic about their forwarding contribution to new life in the galaxy, their hearts were weighed down by an emotion they had not felt in what felt like lifetimes; loss.

The beings missed their friends, missed their friendship and wished to be reunited. But they knew that their purpose lay on a different path, they had to try and find any missing stragglers from their home planet and like any being after a trauma, they had to try and rebuild their lives.

But the little beings knew that they would forever be changed by the love and forgiveness of their friends.

And the Wongtoks would carry those lessons forever forward in their lifetimes.

*

In a bedroom not far from where his friend had committed self-sacrifice, a tall, gangly looking geek surveyed his private living space one final time.

Chilvers touched the photographs of his friends, some still with him, and one now a wondering ghost at the forefront of his mind.

He smiled at his collection of geeky comics, toys and posters and knew that he would never be changed in his soul. He was what he was and he would never apologise for that. He had grown up since the events that had happened all those months ago, his friends had too.

But now he was approaching a threshold in his life that he had to cross.

The safe place he had been accustomed too while teetering on the edge of innocence was now fading into a worn memory.

Chilvers was not afraid to admit that he was terrified of the future; he didn't know what lay ahead. But that was also a little exciting.

He smiled. He took a breath. He closed the door one final time.

The world was still and always would be a little cracked, but it was in those moments where the stories were told. He headed out of his door, not once looking back and in doing so, he let go. He felt his world drown in a sea of pure black and white then slowly melt into a forever darker shade of grey. He knew that he would never get a proper goodbye with his faded friend, he conceded to the notion that sometimes the winds of change blew too briskly over the past, scattering the ashes through the souls of the living, and sometimes, there was nothing you could do about it.

One simply had to adhere to the ghosts of the past, feel them perched on their shoulder every day and answer the promise of tomorrow.

*

In an airport lounge a short distance from his house, Chilvers sat with his two friends. Though they now bore the title of a trio, the geeks kept moving forward. They waited in sweet anticipation of what the new day might bring.

For now, though, they had pressing matters at hand. They were making their first trip outside of their homeland. They each had a ticket that was bound for Los Angeles, California.

Adventure was calling and it had a name.

Harrison Ford.

The boys were to make that lifelong dream come true and Mr. Ford, while doing his part to ease the tension in his hometown during the aftermath of the world war, had gotten wind of the four geeks from the U.K and the endeavour they had fought to save mankind.

Harrison Ford had agreed to fly the boys out to spend a month in America on the set of his latest film. He had also agreed to hold a public memorial for their fallen friend in L.A with some of Hollywood's most sought-after luminaries in attendance.

The geeks had gleefully accepted and so, as they headed for the departure gate, they glanced at the horizon.

The sun was rising.

And a new chapter was beginning.

They knew, with a tinge of sadness, that their stories were only just being told. They were not saying goodbye to their friend, they were simply saying farewell for now.

They would embrace the good times and learn from the bad, and they foreshadowed that they might not always be together but when that day came, they would deal with it as they saw fit.

But not today.

At this very moment, they were together and that was all that mattered. For now, they would keep their minds moving forward, they would keep their eyes trained on the heavens, and they would laugh, they would cry, they would dance in the rain, and they would enjoy themselves at every opportunity.

They would try to face everything that life threw at them with that child-like sense of wonder that had served them so well in the past and who knew...they might just make some memories along the way.

With that in mind, they boarded the plane and jetted off to the land of hopes and dreams. To the land that was home to Harrison Ford.

Though time would move the boys on in its nonchalant manner, the geeks still found themselves forever under the glowing spell of sweet, forgiving childhood friendship.

If they were to be stuck in this void forever, trapped in the lost space between being a child and becoming a man, then that would be okay with them.

The fate of their lifelong friendship had been sealed long ago. They were brothers and it would remain that way until they died. And even then, the echo of a bond tied with blood would forever ricochet through the stars.

ACKNOWLEDGMENTS

The author would like to thank the following people for their unwavering support:

To my Mother and Father, words aren't enough. No son could ask for anything more. I love you both.

To my Nan, where would any of the grandchildren be without you? I love you.

To my comedy colleague Sam, for sharing the stage with you is a sheer joy.

To my dear friend James, for always believing and pushing me.

To my blood brother Andy, for his undying friendship, love and laughter.

To Matt, more like a brother than a cousin.

And to the rest of these constants in the world; Bev and John, Aunties and Uncles, friends who are like family, stand-up friends, old and new friends, extended family, cousins and general good people in the world.

For those I can't thank in person as they are lighting up the heavens, I carry you with me.

And finally; to you the reader. I hope from the bottom of my heart that you enjoyed reading this book as much as I have enjoyed writing it. I hope, if nothing else, that it put a smile on your face.

That's all I ever wanted.

Keep your inner child alive. The world needs it.

Over and out.

Printed in Great Britain
by Amazon